KENT

Edited by Jenni Bannister

First published in Great Britain in 2016 by:

 Young**Writers**

Remus House
Coltsfoot Drive
Peterborough
PE2 9BF
Telephone: 01733 890066
Website: www.youngwriters.co.uk
All Rights Reserved
Book Design by Ashley Janson
© Copyright Contributors 2016
SB ISBN 978-1-78624-123-8

Printed and bound in the UK by BookPrintingUK
Website: www.bookprintinguk.com

FOREWORD

Enter, Reader, if you dare...

For as long as there have been stories there have been ghost stories. Writers have been trying scare their readers for centuries using just the power of their imagination. For Young Writers' latest competition Spine-Chillers we asked students to come up with their own spooky tales, but with the tricky twist of using just 100 words!

They rose to the challenge magnificently and this resulting collection of haunting tales will certainly give you the creeps! From friendly ghosts and Halloween adventures to the gruesome and macabre, the young writers in this anthology showcase their creative writing talents.

Here at Young Writers our aim is to encourage creativity and to inspire a love of the written word, so it's great to get such an amazing response, with some absolutely fantastic stories. We will now choose the top 5 authors across the competition, who will each win a Kindle Fire.

I'd like to congratulate all the young authors in *Spine-Chillers - Kent* - I hope this inspires them to continue with their creative writing. And who knows, maybe we'll be seeing their names alongside Stephen King on the best seller lists in the future...

Jenni Bannister

Editorial Manager

CONTENTS

BETHS GRAMMAR SCHOOL, BEXLEY

BORDEN GRAMMAR SCHOOL, SITTINGBOURNE

GOLDWYN PLUS, ASHFORD

HIGH WEALD ACADEMY, CRANBROOK

LANGLEY PARK SCHOOL FOR BOYS, BECKENHAM

ST GEORGE'S CE SCHOOL, GRAVESEND

THE HUNDRED OF HOO ACADEMY, ROCHESTER

WEST HEATH SCHOOL, SEVENOAKS

THE MINI SAGAS

THE SILENT MADHOUSE

I crept along the decayed stone path. My body was tense and my kneecaps shuddered. *Where is he?* I thought. The night fell silent and the full moon rose to the sky. My squad was meant to be here three hours ago. As I looked up, my eyes came across a grand house. 'They must be in here.'
I had waited in the house for half an hour so I decided to be brave and sleep there for the night. As I lay, the walls whispered to me. Then the truth dawned on me. Lights flashed and I heard screams...

MUSA KAZIM (11)
Beths Grammar School, Bexley

DARKWOOD MANOR

So here it was, in all its glory. Darkwood Manor. Dusty and creaky roof tiles fell onto the empty porch. As I entered, a shiver ran down my spine. But I had to find it... my mother's necklace. Countless memories were in there. Flesh and bones covered the floor. 'Twinkle, twinkle little star,' I whimpered like a coward. I wish Tom was with me. He would know how to calm me down. The feeling of death lingered around me like a reaper's hook. Then I heard it, a whirring chainsaw in all of the rooms surrounding me. I ran.

JAYEN HALAI (12)
Beths Grammar School, Bexley

In The Shadows

The wind grew stronger and blew his hair across his face. The ground was covered with a thick blanket of white snow and his feet became hard to move. He felt paralysed. The shadow of the figure moved towards the shop before it disappeared out of thin air. Another person disappeared into the shadows. Every night when a person went to the very same old boring shop, they would be consumed by the shadows. Hands of fog would grab the victim before lending the victim to the darkness to die. I approached the shop, not knowing about these events...

ETHAN WATT
Beths Grammar School, Bexley

Stalkers

He didn't know who was behind him. Apprehension filled his body while he pondered about where he was. He was in the middle of nowhere. 'Well, we meet again,' said the voice from a body hidden in the darkness.
'Who are you? Where are you coming from?'
Footsteps from the figure became louder. Terror. How it filled him and was the only thing on his mind. 'After all these years, I have finally found you.'
He didn't know how to respond. He was in a paralysis of fear.
Bang! Bang! The figure walked away. Tom lay down, pleading and begging...

KADI (12)
Beths Grammar School, Bexley

PITCH-BLACK, KIDNAP

Pitch-black nothingness. The best time. The body of Frank Harper lay in a pool of cold blood. The detectives came and searched the alleyways. The worst decision. Their last decision. *Whoosh!* One kidnapped. *Whoosh!* Argh! A strangled cry. They were wary. *Whoosh!* One remaining. *Scratch, scratch!* He felt breathing down his neck. He ran. Faster, faster. He could hear other footsteps behind him. Running, running. *Slice, crack!* Above his shoulders. On his neck was where the blade struck. The last detective sprawled out like a rag doll, landing on his back. The dagger came down. Black...

LEANDROS MICHAELIDES (11)
Beths Grammar School, Bexley

THE MYSTERIOUS MAN

Fog creeps in through the window. Now I can't see and there's a slight creaking noise every five seconds. It's getting faster, louder now. I'll call Jane. 'Can you come to my house?' There was no answer. Suddenly, there was a smash, shards of glass cracked into smithereens and the footsteps became closer, louder. A large waft of wind hits me with force, sending me backwards. My heart's beating faster now and I'm breathing heavily. 'Somebody help me!' Someone's breathing on me now, deeply, heavily. Now it's touching me. A freezing arm that's burning my skin. I look up...

BERNIE HOLT (11)
Beths Grammar School, Bexley

One Little Dare...

The door slowly groaned open. Blood was coursing through my
body and my heart was thumping against my chest. I cursed myself
as I stepped into the hallway. Just a stupid little dare and now look
where I'd ended up! I looked back at my friends and three mocking
faces stared back at me. I gulped and cautiously stepped forward.
A powerful smell of musk invaded my nose, instantly repelling me
backwards. My eyes clouded with the shrapnel and dust particles in
the air. That's when I saw it... I felt a withered hand on my shoulder...

JOYAL SHAJAN (11)
Beths Grammar School, Bexley

The Vampire

I looked left, I looked right, nothing was coming. I started walking
across the road. *Smack!* Something had hit me! The next second, I
was rushing to the hospital in the back of an ambulance. I opened
my eyes and all was black. I closed, then opened my eyes again and
all was fine. I saw my mum standing there. *Bang!* My mum fell dead
on the floor. I got up and looked around. Then I saw him, the Devil.
The vampire, with blood-red eyes he stared at me. He lunged forward
at me...

STEPHEN READ (11)
Beths Grammar School, Bexley

Who Creeps In?

Skim! Skam! Shaggy, filthy mice rattle the table. The sound of a creepy atmosphere fills the air. With tension, I observe in detail my surroundings. *Bang! Crash!* Downstairs I hear my pans shaking. Goosebumps start to form throughout my body. 'Hello?' I shout and my echo repeats five times. Suddenly, I look around with my teddy bear in my hand. Gloomy shadows surround my room. I look down at my teddy bear, but where has it gone? A human-like form comes in creepily.
'Argh!'
'Ha! Yum! Who shall I eat next for dinner?'

SUFYAAN JAVED (11)
Beths Grammar School, Bexley

The Dark Knight

It was a cold evening. Josh was walking home from an eventful day. He had been playing golf with his father. As he made his way home, he felt that he was being followed. He slowly turned his head around, but no one was there. He carried on walking then suddenly, he was grabbed round the mouth and was taken hostage! He frantically tried to get away but it was no use. He was taken to an abandoned house where the dark knight revealed himself. It was none other than Josh's dad! Josh's face was expressionless!

LOUIS LEECH (11)
Beths Grammar School, Bexley

Stalking Sword

Slowly, gradually, walking up the creaking staircase. It was hard to imagine that I had lived in this house once. Gazing into my sister's room, my face lost all colour. There was nothing, nothing but a still body. Tears rolled down my face and onto the vibrating floor! Swiftly turning my head, I saw what haunts me even now, what will someday be the death of me. I saw it... the floating sword, pointing its razor-sharp point at me and watching my every move. Slowly, gradually, I got up, confused, dazzled and, not losing all will to live, I ran...

William Taylor (11)
Beths Grammar School, Bexley

Midnight Moon...

The pencil rubbing against the paper was like a chainsaw obliterating wood. I anticipated that something was bound to kick off. Mr Canock entered... yet it wasn't him. My hands were sweating like a waterfall. He started to approach, slower and slower. 'Join us, the dead!' he screamed in anger. I ran, not knowing where to. *Am I safe?*
I thought I was safe then reality struck me like a lightning bolt.
I appeared to be outside a church. The church was engulfed with singing. I dared to enter. I was greeted by menacing Devil worshipers...

Sanam Gill (12)
Beths Grammar School, Bexley

DOLLS

The parade of hills danced as snow created layer after layer of white. The once perfect blue sky incinerated into a ghastly red.
I'd washed the blood off carefully and started wandering around. Killing was fun. It took a few hours before stumbling across that pathetic being. Now, I only wanted a few possible thousand lives to add to my kill count. Wait, she hadn't died!
Hours passed... her hand shone white then blue. She shivered uncontrollably. Hypothermia. She had been stabbed by a doll. Impossible! She walked slowly. There she was, standing. 'Hello again.'
Her hope faded away.

KOSAR BABANI (11)
Beths Grammar School, Bexley

OVER AND OUT

Creak! The door suddenly threw open rapidly. Nobody was there. 'Argh!' The scream sent a cold shiver down my spine. A child then pelted down the corridor. I heard loud, ear-busting footsteps heading straight for me. It was Mr Doust, my English teacher. 'You will recede.' Unexpectedly, a cupboard fell... I was netted. Demon Doust lifted up the cupboard as if it wasn't even heavy and then chained the door. I was powerless and unable to exit. The cupboard was then abruptly discarded over the window ledge. Subsequently, I heard a woman's voice in my head...

HARUN ABDUL RAHMAN (11)
Beths Grammar School, Bexley

Unconscious

The leaves shifted violently. Tom looked around the area, swivelling his eyes cautiously. All was still. The wind was howling more viciously now, so he had to find shelter. At last, he saw an old and isolated shop. The lights had gone out. The power must have gone.
Boom! Someone must have shut the door. He was trying to get the optimistic feeling that it was just the wind. Was it? Now he was trembling like a worn-out washing machine.
He felt a cold, menacing hand on his trembling shoulders. Was it the end?

RICHARD PAUL (11)
Beths Grammar School, Bexley

They're Back

I knew they'd be after me again. I thought it would be much longer before they came, but when I heard them, I knew they were back. The clock ticked and tocked before they came. The ancient kettle made the rusty, high-pitched drone. *Bang!*
The invasion started! I felt my heart stop before I heard the cries of civilians. The church bell chimed. Near the crumbling school building children were being silently assassinated by the black figures and I knew I was next.
So I ran...

EDEN LENNON
Beths Grammar School, Bexley

THE HORROR OF THE HOLLOWS

I ran when I heard the screech of the creature, the hollow. These hollows are demons, preying on souls who watch the dancing of the leaves in the dead of the night. 'Help!' I shouted but I knew nobody would reply. This was it, my only refuge being a shack, so I ran and shut the door, using all my strength to keep the hollow out. The shrieks were gone. I slipped down to the floor, my back against the door, feeling happy, thinking that I had survived.
The sun came up, I then turned round to see the horror...

RHYS ROCHA (11)
Beths Grammar School, Bexley

STUCK!

He stopped running. Sweat dripped and fell down. Breathing heavily, he started walking. Did he lose them? 'Let me call Jack and see if he can take me home.' Looking behind, he slowly got his phone out. *Ring, ring, ring.* What was that sound? He looked around the corner and there it was... blood dripping from its disgusting, horrendous, terrifying mouth. It had yellow eyes glaring straight at him. 'Run, run!' whispered the air. He was struck frozen in fear. Its eyes looked hungrily at him. *Bang!* They found him. The bullet missed him. Then he saw Jack, dead.

JOSEPH SEKAMWA (12)
Beths Grammar School, Bexley

THE MYSTERIOUS LIGHT

It all started on a gloomy night after school. On the way home there was a weird light coming from the bushes. I'd been in detention and had missed my bus, so why not go in. There was a sign saying, *Do Not Enter*. I looked around and saw community police. I quickly jumped in when they weren't looking. Sitting inside there was a shadow, no body, just a shadow and a crystal ball. I touched it and a ghostly figure appeared with a sinister smile. I turned to run, but there was no way.
'I've got you now.'

OLIVER BOWDERY (11)
Beths Grammar School, Bexley

THE SMALL TOWN

In a small, isolated town, a tragedy occurred four years ago. A malevolent man engulfed houses in flames. Every year he comes back to the town. Tonight, an unfortunate man had been chosen to watch the town's outskirts for the person.
As night fell and the sky darkened, a flash of lightning revealed a figure approaching the town. The man's heart sank to his shoes and he started to breathe quickly. The wind started to howl and trees started to rustle. Suddenly, an icy-cold hand gripped his shoulder and he fell to the ground, dead.

ROBERT VOUILLEMIN (12)
Beths Grammar School, Bexley

THE OLD WELL

I fell down the old well. Fortunately, I wasn't hurt. At the bottom there was a skeleton, a horrid thing in the tatters of a summer dress. I was terrified. I climbed out and ran back to the hospital but I couldn't find my mum, only a man and a woman I didn't know. I approached them. The man ignored me, but the woman screamed and then I realised there was something important I'd forgotten. Then I was back in the dark well again with that horrible skeleton. *What have I forgotten? What was it? And where's my mum?*

GAREN ANIGHORO (12)
Beths Grammar School, Bexley

DON'T WAKE UP

Thomas woke up, for the third time tonight. He was thirsty, so he went downstairs. He poured himself a glass of orange juice and turned around to go back to bed. The next thing he saw made him freeze on the spot. 'Don't wake up' written on the wall. He ran. He reached his bed. He fell asleep for hours, days, maybe months, then he woke up. He was chained to a chair, sitting in a white room. There was a ghostly figure sitting in front of him with clear, red words behind him. 'You woke up'. It was over.

SANDY MORRISON (12)
Beths Grammar School, Bexley

SQUAD 13

America, 1964. War. Squad 13 are on patrol late at night. They're on the lookout for any enemy activity. 'Sir! John! He's dead!' cried Gary. 'What?' replied the captain. 'Bill, James, check it out!'
'Yes, sir,' they said. They left.
Ten minutes later...
'Sir, there was nothing there!' said Bill.
'Check again!' commanded the captain.
They didn't return. 'Run,' the captain said calmly.
Gary dropped dead.
'Run!' they all yelled.
They hadn't got ten metres before two more died. The captain backed away. He turned. He saw a pale man. The man plunged his hand into the captain's chest...

LUKE JEFKINS (12)
Beths Grammar School, Bexley

Beware Of The Woods

It was Halloween. Tim was excited. He had a schedule and was determined to stick with it. *Ding-dong!* Joseph was early. Tim and Joseph had been best friends for 12 years. They were going trick or treating together, but that was the last time they ever saw each other...

It was on the news that they travelled through the woods to save time. However, they never came out.

Ten years later, in 2006, two more boys went in the woods and never came out, so beware, because in 2016 more boys will go missing. Don't go near Bexley Woods!

Joseph Kocabas (12)
Beths Grammar School, Bexley

The Bus Stop Mystery

One day, Tom was coming back home from school, along with his mate Charlie. When they were waiting in the bus stop, they heard a slight rumble, although they later assumed it was nothing to worry about. Later, when Charlie said goodbye to Tom, Tom walked to the nearest bus stop along with many others, mainly schoolchildren. But suddenly, he heard a rumble, an even louder one than before. Once again, Tom thought that it was nothing to worry about. When he was getting off the bus, as well as an ear-splitting rumble, something grabbed him ferociously...

Victor Ezeja (12)
Beths Grammar School, Bexley

THE RIVER

This story starts in Bexley, my school in fact. Every games lesson we trek across to another field, over a bridge. On our first lesson, one kid was dared to wade through the river. He accepted. One step, fine. Two steps, fine. But suddenly, the silt and stones appeared to grab his ankles! He screamed, but when our coach arrived, his arm was dragged under. Nobody's heard anything since, until someone ventured under to retrieve a football. The original boy's face was printed on the underside of the bridge. The man could tell no more. They were both missing.

ADAM COLLEN (11)
Beths Grammar School, Bexley

CHAINS

'Marley! I'm here. Hello?' No reply. *Slash! Bang, bang!* They were in the mansion. Well, Marley was until...
Jamie saw things that didn't need to be seen. There were gravestones everywhere. The only thing that was wrong was that they had chains on. Now, gravestones are meant to be outside... these weren't. Jamie dared herself to go touch them. She was ready. She walked up to the graves, lifted the chains up and got a nasty surprise. *Clang!* She screamed. A man came into the mansion. 'It's over now, so don't fear.'
'What are you?' she said.
'The keeper,' he replied.

NATHANIEL OYESANYA (11)
Beths Grammar School, Bexley

THE DEATH NOTE

Charlie, the boy who was unaware of what destruction he was about to cause, veered into an alleyway. But the thing kept following. It radiated an aura of gloom and death. We only know this because he wrote it on the wall of his death zone. Death followed him although Charlie wanted it least. The death note had been released because of telling what it's like. Now it'll rain its tyranny on all of us when we least want it. It'll follow you and it's inevitable. It will do its deed. Each kill is one step closer to you. RIP.

ARNAV UPADHYAYA (11)
Beths Grammar School, Bexley

THE HITCHHIKER

Fifty years ago, several sightings were reported of a poltergeist. This is just one of them. Two men in a car, driving in the countryside. That sounds nice, doesn't it? Birds tweeting, bliss. These two men suddenly noticed a woman plodding up the road. These men assumed her to be a hitchhiker and presumed the hiker to be in dire need of a lift. So, being the kind young men they were, helped her clamber inside. Once she was in and secure, they set off, feeling pleased with themselves for helping. They turned for a conversation... she wasn't there.

JOSHUA MCWILLIAMS (12)
Beths Grammar School, Bexley

The Night Creeper

It was night and the fog was wrapping itself around me. I strode forward, listening to the hoots of owls. Suddenly, a hoot was cut short. A gurgling shriek broke the silence. Instantly, I was running. I heard footsteps pound behind me. Quickly, a cold, pale hand struck my neck. As I tumbled, I looked up only to see a large, ominous silhouette. Two purple eyes stared at me, penetrating my soul and killing me from inside. A hand grasped me by the neck. I felt myself rise and choke. Then I saw a white light, such bright white light...

Maciek Stepien (12)
Beths Grammar School, Bexley

The Hand

Knock! Knock! I was in my room doing homework. *Knock! Knock!* There it was again. 'Go away, Sam.' There was no reply. *Knock! Knock!* 'Go away!' I turned, looking in the direction of the door, expecting to see my brother's face. There was a hand, only a hand, a hand drowned in blood! I was petrified. I turned, hoping it would evaporate! But no. *Knock! Knock!* It was moving closer. *Knock! Knock!* Getting closer. Then it stopped. It was replaced by a sound so horrible! I turned with the desire to make it halt. That was a mistake...

Ben Aldred
Beths Grammar School, Bexley

The Orphanage

Thunderstorm clouds gathered intently. Rain began to fall rapidly. A storm was nigh. As I ran homeward, I couldn't help but think of what a horrid thing I had just done. Thoughts flooded into my mind with quickness. Those poor, helpless children. How could I?
Running, running, I couldn't stop. Ouch, my head, it hurt so much. I couldn't stop myself. The consequences, what would happen? Would they find my fingerprints or the blood? The footsteps were becoming louder, at a quicker pace. I was so, so afraid. The pale faces of those children would haunt me, even in death.

CONOR MELVILLE (12)
Beths Grammar School, Bexley

Dark Eyes

It was behind me, I could feel it. Those eyes, those dark eyes burning holes into my skin. I couldn't see them, but I knew they were there. Circling me, watching me.
'Anna? Where are you? Please come back, I didn't mean it.'
Those eyes, closer, closer.
'Anna? Help!'
Closer.
All the muscles in my body tensed. Then a cold hand on my shoulder.
The next day, a girl was sprawled on the floor, throat ripped out, in pools of blood. The owner of the eyes was still hunting...

OLIVER PETCH (11)
Beths Grammar School, Bexley

GOODNIGHT, DAVID JOHNSON

David had been alone for three days now, neglected in the bungalow. He lay upon his bunk bed, listening to the sound of traffic. Now another sound came from outside, this sound within ten feet of the bungalow. Like everything else, David ignored it and rolled back into bed. The sound appeared again, seeming so close yet so far. Now it all happened. The windows were smashed in, leaving David surrounded with shattered glass. A figure climbed in, its face hidden behind a black veil. David screamed his last. 'Goodnight, David Johnson' read the letter upon him.
Goodnight, David Johnson.

OLIVER GABRIEL TOMLINSON (11)
Beths Grammar School, Bexley

CRIES OF SADNESS

I was there standing, waiting for my bus, but it didn't come. I was the only one there, I was the only one on the street. I wanted to leave but something was stopping me. I heard faint cries of sadness. I was scared. I cried for help, there was no answer. I tried to call 911, there was no answer. Then I heard footsteps, loud footsteps. I could see a figure in the distance covered in a dark suit. I fainted. The last thing I remember is that on the bus, blood was trickling down my neck...

JOSHUA MUIRURI (11)
Beths Grammar School, Bexley

The Hunt

I was running, the rain pattering on my head. I ran past the hands of trees, begging for one of the branches to trap the monstrous creature. I skidded past a tree, falling in the process. A branch imbedded in my thigh. However, this was the least of my worries. 'Help!' The rain acted as a visor. I couldn't see anything. I got up, blood flowing out of my thigh, causing a red puddle. The trees whispered for me to hide. I dived into a prickly bush of thorns. I heard a piercing growl. Will I ever see tomorrow's sun?

GEORGE PALMER (11)
Beths Grammar School, Bexley

You Will Never Escape

We were walking back from school on a cold, misty day. It all happened at once. We were talking when out of a gloomy, heart-pounding, terrifying alleyway, a crazed psychopath came swinging a bloody knife. I turned to Alex to run, but it all happened so quickly. The next thing I knew I was on the floor while Alex was throwing his arms and legs everywhere. I tried with all my might to get up and save Alex, but I was almost dead. I heard running. I turned my head. Alex was gone...

JACK BOSWELL (11)
Beths Grammar School, Bexley

The Big Surprise

The sound of footsteps woke me up with a jolt! I slowly crept to the light and flicked the switch. There was no light! I crawled back to my bed, totally spooked. *Tap, tap.* There it was again! Now I felt like screaming. *Creak!* went the door. 'Hello?' I called. 'Is anyone there?' No reply. I started to panic so I plucked up all my courage to go check it out! As I opened my bedroom door, to my horror I saw blood splattered all over the wall! Then I felt something on my left shoulder. 'Hello?' Slowly I turned...

OLIVER MEGGS (11)
Beths Grammar School, Bexley

Jack's Uncle

Jack hated his uncle. His uncle never spoke to anyone. Nobody knew anything about him. Every week he went out with his friends. But one night, he didn't come back. Hours passed - still no sign of his uncle. Jack started to tremble. Where could he be? He went outside. 'Uncle?' called Jack. No answer. He walked down the street. 'Uncle?' he called again.
'Yes,' said a figure behind him.
'Argh!' screamed Jack.
'You shouldn't have come,' said the figure. 'Goodbye, Jack.'
Jack felt a cold, sharp blade in his stomach. He knew it was all over for him.

JAMES GUEST (11)
Beths Grammar School, Bexley

THE TOMBSTONE SHED

Here's a thriller about a shed...
Marley and I were exploring the shed behind school that was rumoured to be haunted. Marley begged to go home. I dared him to go into the shed for two minutes. Then (using a plank) slammed the door. Marley instantly came running out screaming, even though I didn't start. I explored for myself and the door closed. Courageously, I looked around until I found a block of stone. Wait. 'Is that... ' Before I could finish, the ceiling collapsed on me. All I remember it saying was 'RIP Jason Booker'.

JONATHAN JOSEPH-IYANDA (11)
Beths Grammar School, Bexley

THE KNIGHT OF DEATH

Once there lived a knight called Harrison. He served the king with great honour, but even the greatest can be killed. It was a cold winter night, casting menacing shadows across the face of the Earth. The knight was taking a nice leisurely stroll down Caster Road when *bang!* Some crates fell. *Whoosh!* A flaming arrow went whizzing above his head. 'Hello?' exclaimed the knight.
'Ra!' responded a shadow.
'What the... ?'
That sentence was never finished because at that very moment a black image went and ate him whilst ripping his spine out.

MICHAEL MASON-MAHON (11)
Beths Grammar School, Bexley

The Beginning Of The End

Drip, drip, drip. It was a cold, gloomy night in the depths of Elm Street, otherwise known as the road of mystery. It was so quiet that you could even hear the scuttling of woodlice. Suddenly, the radio started to babble, the wind howled in agony. Simultaneously, loud, ear-bursting screeches came from outside the now shattered window along with faint growls from the other side of the door. Frozen in terror, shivers sped down my spine. All I could do was wait, hope that this would stop. It didn't. I realised that this was just the beginning of the end.

Joao Pedro Castro Pires (12)
Beths Grammar School, Bexley

Left Behind

I was walking with the others: Tom, Jerry and Bugs. We were in the old, haunted hospital when a bang was heard. We ran as fast as we could. I knew I wouldn't be able to catch up with the others so I made for the nearest closet and prayed silently. I waited and waited. Roughly an hour had passed. I heard what sounded like three footsteps. 'Where do you think she is?' whispered a voice which sounded like nobody I knew. Going against my better judgement, I stepped out face-to-face with nothing. Suddenly, blood dripped...

Yasin Ali (12)
Beths Grammar School, Bexley

KEEP OUT

It was 10pm. Lee waited at the bus stop. An elderly woman approached the stop. 'Hello, child.' Lee nodded to her while looking at his new smartphone. 'You kids and your technology.' The woman's purse fell onto the ground. 'Can you pick that up for me?'
Lee bent down to pick it up for the lady. When he stood up, nobody was there. He said, 'Hello, is anybody there?' When there was no response, he peered into the purse and attempted to grab the belongings of the lady. Suddenly, he froze as a faint voice whispered, 'Keep out!'

ASANTE SIAW (11)
Beths Grammar School, Bexley

NIGHTMARE IN AFGHANISTAN

2013, Afghanistan. A night patrol was scanning the perimeter.
'Sure is dark out here,' said the commander.
'Yeah, you can't see anything,' said leader Roy.
They carried on walking with the sound of bullets in the air. Then they stopped. 'Commander, there are two green flashing lights.'
'OK. Me, James and Jackson will check it out.'
They started walking towards the lights with curiosity. When they were near, James shone his torch at them. 'Oh, it's just a wild fox.' He turned to give the thumbs up, when the ground crumbled beneath them and they fell into an endless trap...

GEORGE CLARK (11)
Beths Grammar School, Bexley

DEATH SENTENCE

The clouds came in vast numbers, covering up the sun. I was walking slowly. Suddenly, a huge tree stump was in front of me and I fell over. My mind went blank. I woke up in a dark building, got up and walked outside. I was in a graveyard. One grave caught my eye. It said 'Ethan King 2002-2015'. My name is Ethan King and I was born in 2002. A cold hand clasped my shoulder, a death angel. 'Is this some kind of stupid joke?' I shouted.
The death angel nodded solemnly. 'You've been dead for four hours.'

JOSHUA POOLE (12)
Beths Grammar School, Bexley

THE GNOME

It was an eerie, dark night. Sitting perched upon the balcony that overshadowed the pond, was an oversized gnome. Cute on the outside, but a bloodthirsty demon on the inside. That very gnome-like demon was situated in Darkwood Manor. 'This looks fairy intriguing. Shall we go in?' questioned Bob to his best friend, Jim.
Jim replied, 'Yes,' and so they did.
Their first obstacle was the front garden. That was the only obstacle they were going to encounter. They failed to hurdle it. The gnome, that is all that needs to be said.

FINLEY TRIVETT (11)
Beths Grammar School, Bexley

FLASH OF HOPE

Crack! Boom! The barricade wouldn't hold out for Kyle. The bug-infected people would break through. Unfortunately, there were too many for modified kitchen utensils. How did this happen? Only five days ago he was watching Hollyoaks when the first one appeared through the window.

Suddenly, devastating screams awoke him from his flashback, the other survivors across the street were no more. Alarmingly, the window yet again blew to shards. He stabbed and slashed, but he was one, they were most of London!

Suddenly, light beamed through and a flash of hope appeared, but it soon went, with the car!

JAMES BEARDOW (11)
Beths Grammar School, Bexley

THE BEGINNING OF THE WORLD'S DESTRUCTION

James woke up. He suddenly felt the urge to go outside.

When James was exploring his garden, the nose of a jet picked him up and raced at 10,000 miles per hour. Suddenly, the jet was shot and he had found himself hanging with his last bit of hope, when something touched him. Then the world froze and everything turned white. The creature was smiling.

Suddenly, he had woken up where everything was gone. He was flying to another planet which was red and was moving. When he was metres away, he got sucked up and there was the monster...

LAKSHAN SENTHILKUMARAN (11)
Beths Grammar School, Bexley

THE BED MONSTER

'Dad! There's something under my bed!' a girl with blonde hair, blue eyes and called Amy shouted. This naive 6-year-old was living a rather peculiar life. Random rattles and hisses devoured the dark, minute house, but the bed monster? Amy's parents both thought it was a made-up figure.
'No there isn't!' Amy's dad replied.
'Check!' Amy backfired with a frail face.
Her dad checked. Nothing was found except fur! Fur? Spontaneously, a warm, moist breath ran down his neck and an abnormally tall shadow appeared.
'Dad! It's behind you!'

RAFIAD ULLAH (11)
Beths Grammar School, Bexley

The Church Of Shadows

The priest smirked as he ambled past me. His intimidating, yet spine-chilling, presence instantly made me shiver. *Oooze! Drip!* I spun around. The exit was etched with the words 'doom is your forsaken fate'. I suddenly had the urge to turn back around. As I did, I glared at something that must have been a nightmare. In the former position of the priest stood an ambiguous creature. His torso was completely pitch-black and he definitely wasn't 3D. Or was he? I rubbed my eyes to check if I wasn't awake, but I was and it was reaching out...

Dolapo Seriki (12)
Beths Grammar School, Bexley

Mist

There it was, in front of me. I wouldn't really call it a ghost but more an ashy mist. It blended in with the night sky, except for two sinister eyes. It was moving though, squelching sounds with every step it made. Then... its pace quickened, singing, crying, prancing this spirit-like creature skipped towards me, a girl on a summer's day. Closer with every step, I started sprinting, a heavy backpack on my shoulder, a torch in my hand. I tripped, face-planting onto a rock, blood trickling down my face, gushing, as I looked up...

Ben Thomas (11)
Beths Grammar School, Bexley

THE CURSED ROCKING HORSE

As I entered the eerie room, I switched on the lamp in the corner. I sat down in my chair and picked up my cup of hot chocolate. Suddenly, the room began to darken. The fireplace had gone out and everything was invisible apart from the lamp in the corner. I heard everything in the house shaking as if an earthquake had hit. The fireplace erupted into flames and my prized rocking horse turned its head in a one hundred and eighty degree turn to face me. 'Why?' it questioned me and transformed into a terrible beast. 'Why? Why? Why?'

CHARLIE ANDERSON (11)
Beths Grammar School, Bexley

THE BEDROOM SWITCH

I was playing on my PlayStation in my room, enjoying my favourite games. The light started to flicker, on, off, on, off, so I called Dad to check the bulb. He came, however, the light was fine. 'Just something minor,' said Dad.
When he left, it started again! Only this time there was clicking with it. I turned my console off. But the click was still there. I glanced at the switch, it was moving up and down! Panic filled me when suddenly, *ping!* The bulb burst. I ran. Dad saw me and went to check. The bulb was fine...

KHUNAL HOOLLAH (12)
Beths Grammar School, Bexley

THE GHOSTS OF SPECTRE

Captain Skye stood at the bow of his ship. He was a fearless man who was afraid of nothing. Then he noticed the fog, a blackish-green mist creeping over the horizon. Then he saw it... a flash. Something was coming... a ghostly object coming from the deep. Captain Skye started getting nervous. It was an emerald galleon in the distance. As the vessel drew near, Captain Skye could see ghostly green figures climbing the masts and a blood-red flag hanging from the crow's nest. Captain Skye grabbed a cutlass, but it was too late. The Pirates of Spectre were coming closer...

DANNY MARRIOTT (11)
Beths Grammar School, Bexley

THE MIST

The corridor was empty, yet beckoning with children. I entered the classroom. The majestic moon danced in the pitch-black sky. I struggled to understand the eerie fog coming through the solid wall. I switched on the dim light. Apparently, I've done this before. Suddenly, the fog thickened, but it was still inside the room. As I looked upon the archaic grandfather clock, I saw... time wasn't moving! I abruptly checked my phone to see the message: 'You're never alone'. Unexpectedly, the lights went off and then I saw a pair of ominous blue eyes staring at me...

ROJAN KARKI (11)
Beths Grammar School, Bexley

BLACK POWDER

I remember it all well. Too well. What do I remember though? I shall tell you...
A tornado-like storm crept upon an unsuspecting student (me). Cautiously waiting for a bus, I could sense the choking force of smoke. Cigarettes! Latching onto my clean face, it destroyed my insides. The cloudy mass came from an evil-looking woman. Stupidly, I said, 'Stop!' I had certainly dug a deep hole for myself. The smoke covered my anxious body until I appeared like a dark cumulonimbus. Throwing up, I desperately tried to breathe. Today, I knew I wasn't going home, rather Heaven.

JOSHUA LAWORE (12)
Beths Grammar School, Bexley

THE SWINGS

The swings. Many rumours had spread about them. As soon as you sat on them, either thick fog surrounded you, or an 'incident' happened. This was all running through Jamie's head as he approached them. 'It's all a load of rubbish,' his friends had said. He had believed them. Past tense. Now he wasn't sure. He sat on the old rubber seat and impossibly, thunder struck simultaneously. Thick grey fog had started climbing towards the swings. It carried on. The fog surrounded him. He felt something on his neck. Breath. He turned around, only to find glowing, red eyes...

BEN SKINNER (12)
Beths Grammar School, Bexley

THE ROCKING CHAIR

I'd been convinced that my bedroom was haunted. Cobwebs, a cracked window and a rocking chair. I swore I'd seen it move on its own before. My parents disagreed. One day, I'd prove them wrong. This was the night. I'd set up a camera. I'd catch the mysterious rocker. 'Ahh! Who was that?' The rocking chair was moving. The wardrobe was wobbling. *It must be in there*, I thought. I was too scared to look so I took refuge in the hall. Then the wardrobe stopped moving. In the doorway stood a tall, shadowy figure waiting there. I screamed...

GEORGE WILES (11)
Beths Grammar School, Bexley

YOU CAN'T HURT US NOW

The park. It's where I am. Nine o'clock in the evening, dark shadows falling through the leaves. The soft clicking of insects in the bushes. *Crack!* Suddenly, the clicking is cracking of bones, ripping of flesh. That is when I see them. Large, bloodthirsty crickets intimidating their old masters, the humans. Their long, ragged arms reaching out to rip my flesh. No pleading with our new masters. What we gave to them they give to us. I see my eye on the ground. Death welcomes me with open arms. The insects will take over, when, I do not know.

ADAM PETRYK (11)
Beths Grammar School, Bexley

My Classroom

It all started in a school, in a classroom, mine in fact. Dark clouds were closing in on my town. No one went in; ever. I thought hiding in school overnight would be amusing. I should have reconsidered. Silence, darkness, isolation. It felt that each step I took, something behind followed.

Finally, I made it to my form room, though it felt a bit peculiar or abnormal. Anyway, I was too blinded by the amusement that I didn't notice the horror. The books and tables were crushing at my feet. The last thing I saw was the teacher...

Dawid Mitura (11)
Beths Grammar School, Bexley

The Trunk In The Woods

The grandfather clock struck twelve. Fear shot up Alex's spine. 'Time to get spooked then. Let's go,' he muttered.

Alex arrived in the woods two minutes later. Bill was already there, waiting. 'Ready?' asked Bill.

'I guess,' replied Alex.

'Race ya!' Bill ran off into the moonlit forest of horrors.

'Bill! Wait!' Alex ran, hoping to find Bill. Thirteen crows shot into the sky. Alex reached the clearing. 'Bill?' Thirteen trees surrounded a lonely trunk. 'Bill?' Alex leant over the trunk. There was something there. 'Bill?'

A sinister laugh broke out. 'Out of luck... '

A piercing scream... silence.

Eliot Wardle (12)
Beths Grammar School, Bexley

THE CIRCUS

Joseph was scared. The icy wind chilled his face. Over in the distance, a large red tent stood alone in-between the trees. The moonlight shone through a tear in the roof casting a silver light into the tent. Mangled, unrecognisable, rotting, torn open carcasses filled the air with a deathly stench. The seats had been torn apart and animal faeces stained the floor. Posters, wrecked and ragged, hung from the walls. A cackle echoed in the forgotten darkness. Joseph stumbled onto a podium in the middle. Joseph heard a sound behind him. He felt a hand.
'Shall we play?'

TOMMY ROWLINGSON (12)
Beths Grammar School, Bexley

THE GNOME

It was dark. My brother had tied me up over an hour ago. Clouds began to gather above and it didn't help that my mum's garden gnome was staring at me. I looked around. When I looked to where the gnome had been, it was gone. Snap! I turned to see the gnome behind me. Within seconds, it began to walk towards me. Then it started, 'Ring-a-ring o' roses,' it sang with its arms stretched out in front. 'A pocket full of posies,' it continued. In a second it would be with me. God only knew what it would do...

AARON CARL VILLALTA (12)
Beths Grammar School, Bexley

THE GREEN SEA WITCH

Fog, was slowly creeping upon me. The night was slowly dawning and I knew this park was out of the ordinary. Beads of sweat drizzled down my spine. I knew I was running but I didn't know what from. *Splash!* went a raindrop, *splish!* went another. Buckets of rain poured on my head. Suddenly, a green, swollen, bony, outstretched hand reached for my leg. It dug its filthy, bloodstained fingernails into my skin. I screamed for help, no one answered. I was down to my waist in a green, gooey substance. Down to my neck in this thick substance. I...

VICTOR ADEOLU ADEWUMI (11)
Beths Grammar School, Bexley

THE DEMON WITHIN

'Jimmy, Jimmy!' There was no reply. The trees above sounded as if they were whispering to each other, talking about their next evil plan. Bob followed the path which eventually led to an opening in the trees. Bob squeezed through it to find a cornfield. In the cornfield was a scarecrow. Its button eyes were looking straight into Bob's own eyes. *Snap!* Bob suddenly heard something behind him. He turned. There was nothing. He looked back. The scarecrow had vanished, completely vanished. Not knowing what had happened, Bob sprinted into the cornfield, blind to what was about to happen...

HARRY NUNES (11)
Beths Grammar School, Bexley

THE OLD OAK TREE

Midnight struck. Mikey still didn't go to the toilet and I was so cold I thought parts of me would start falling off. Mysteriously, I heard a high ringing sound in my ears and Mikey and everyone else disappeared. Only one single oak tree was now visible. Then suddenly, night started to turn to day and I fell into a trance. Everything was engulfed in a deep fog - the grass was dying, the sky grew darker, the air got colder and the oak grew taller and taller until everything stopped. The ringing, the night and day cycled overhead. I collapsed.

BART SALYGA (12)
Beths Grammar School, Bexley

THE PARK

Black clouds smothered the moon, sending Bexley into darkness. I ran down the street towards the gloomy park. The two lamps in the centre flickered with light. Shadows played against the trees. This confused me as there wasn't anyone else there. I crept further in. The light went out altogether. There was rustling coming from all directions. Shadows loomed in front of me. I ran but stumbled and fell to the muddy ground. Figures came closer towards me. They were speaking... it almost sounded like they were chanting something. I couldn't make out the words. Then a hand grabbed me...

LAWRENCE COLEMAN (11)
Beths Grammar School, Bexley

THE PHILOSOPHER'S STONE

I trudged through the hollow woods, thinking about what I was doing. It was a terrible experience. I kept on walking and trudging and marching. Then, I heard a noise. It was a wolf howling, as loud as it could possibly howl. After what seemed like an hour, but was only five minutes, I realised there was a hut and in that hut was a stone. Not just any stone, the philosopher's stone. It shone more brightly than ever. I went to pick it up. It gave me a shock, an electric shock, which was absolutely shocking!

LEON ONYANGO (11)
Beths Grammar School, Bexley

THE CHASE

The bullets sprayed behind me, I could hear them clanking against the blue containers as I ran. I could smell the salt of the sea... then a sudden pain in my leg made me stumble. I had been pierced by a bullet! I knew I had to get myself to safety or I'd be a goner! So I picked myself up off the ground and limped slowly off to one side into an open container. I slammed the door shut and backed into the shadows. The next thing I knew, I was slumped on the container floor, seemingly knocked out!

SAMUEL THARBY (11)
Beths Grammar School, Bexley

Whispers

The trees were talking.
They were always whispering. Hidden secrets lurk in their trunks, on their branches. I scrambled through the woods, tripping on roots and snagging my ragged clothes on branches. I didn't know where I was going, only which direction.
Away from The Grove.
Now I could hear them passing on the message, from tree to tree, closer and closer.
I wasn't fast enough. I wasn't going to make it.
The whispers were catching up. Now they filled my ears. I couldn't keep going. The Grove was going to suck me back.
The Grove doesn't let secrets go...

JAY ENNIS (12)
Beths Grammar School, Bexley

The Night

The night was dark. I stumbled through the forest looking for safety. Although I was travelling as fast as I could, I feared it was catching up. Dan screamed in terror. He fell down behind me. I was the only one left from the original four of us who had started the journey. They had all been caught. Then I saw it, out the corner of my eye. I noticed a derelict farmhouse about 400 metres down the muddy track.
When I arrived, I dashed through the unlocked door unaware of the consequences that I was yet to suffer...

GEORGE BISHOP (11)
Beths Grammar School, Bexley

The Incoming Noises

I was in my house when suddenly, I heard a creak at the door.
I called out, saying, 'Hello!' No reply. I called again. This time I
received a spooky response, something like, 'I'm coming!' All of a
sudden, I heard the sound of a knife followed by a scream. I began
to run away. I thought I was safe until I heard footsteps and I began
to scream. 'Aarrgh!' It was getting closer and I kept running, then I
tripped over some wood. I woke up, I thought to myself, *it's a dream.*
Then I heard a sound.
'Argh!'

Daniel Moulton (11)
Beths Grammar School, Bexley

Mister?

I woke up. I felt breathing on my hand. I opened my eyes. I was in
the middle of nowhere. There was tall grass surrounding me, that
was all I could see. I turned around. I saw a giant-sized crow. It
squawked an ear-splitting squawk. It lifted me with its talons, up
and up. It suddenly dropped me and I landed on a mattress in the
middle of the night in London. I saw someone around the corner.
'Mister!' I yelled as I ran. He wasn't there. I was scared and started to
hyperventilate. I realised what was happening.

Matthew Gainsford (12)
Beths Grammar School, Bexley

THE SCREAMS

The screams, oh the screams.
Lights flicker as I clamber through the darkness.
The screams, oh the screams.
The frost was like a blade on my face. A cool zephyr wafts through the orchard as I dart through the clutches of hell.
The screams, oh the screams.
Heart pounding, blood rising, suddenly I stop. I fall to my knees. Silence. Suddenly, the world comes to an end around me. Crisp leaves crumble underneath, footsteps. Someone or something is approaching. Out of the blue, a sharp pain in my spine. I hear a whisper.
Oh, the screams...

BENJAMIN DE LANGE (12)
Beths Grammar School, Bexley

SHADOWS

She got out of her car and started running. He had tricked her into meeting here. The night sky was overcast and not a single star could penetrate the cloud cover. He was catching her, the blade of his knife flashing in the moonlight. She ran further then further into the dark wood, but alas, the blade cut through her cold skin. But no one would hear her last cry as she fell amongst the whispering grass. He could hear the sirens coming, but he disappeared into the shadows.

OLIWIER SWEDROWSKI (11)
Beths Grammar School, Bexley

THE GRAVES

The night was darker than black. The wind whipped around my cheek. James was with me as I walked through the crumbling gravestones. Suddenly, lots of groaning noises came from the graves. I looked for James, but I couldn't see him. I was paralysed with fear. The ground started to erupt as withered, skeletal hands appeared. I screamed and started to run, but the hands stopped me. They emerged from the ground to form full skeletons. The skeletons started to walk towards me and grabbed me. I tried to get free but I couldn't. I knew it was the end.

JOSEPH TRANTER (11)
Beths Grammar School, Bexley

SHADOW

Shadowy tendrils swum around the old, abandoned warehouse, devouring the cars that came every once in a while. Darkness descended like a falling skydiver, as I made my way through the depressing graveyard, taking the short cut home. Lights flickered on and off by a nearby bar. A crow sounded off in the background, screaming... when I saw a person in the distance. I rubbed my eyes, no one usually came around here. I looked back... no one was there. Then I realised the 'fog' wasn't fog. Hundreds of hands reached for me. I closed my eyes, and ran...

RAHIB IMTIAZ (12)
Beths Grammar School, Bexley

Is Death Waiting?

My heart skipped a beat. The ice-cold wind blew in my pale face. Small snowflakes fell in front of me. I wouldn't make it. An abandoned cottage lay in front of my bright blue eyes. The wind was so strong I had to go in the cottage. I knocked once on the wooden door. Nobody came. The door opened. I entered. I thought I would stay the night. I lay down on a sofa. The dark shadows from old furniture gave me goosebumps. Suddenly, a shadow moved. I scanned the room. Suddenly, a small hand gently tapped me...

Ignacio Góngora Arche (11)
Beths Grammar School, Bexley

Highway To Hell

The wind was like a flat blade of ice. The fog covered up roads so much, even screams couldn't be heard! Brian and Emma had just come from a nightclub and were drunk. Brian was driving illegally and crazily. He paced it on the highway but didn't see the figure ahead in time. Rapidly stopping, the figure walked to the car. The fog crept in; Brian opened the window... A few seconds later, there was a muffled scream followed by a gunshot.
'Brian!' Emma exclaimed. 'Is this a joke?'
The figure shadowed menacingly above her. 'You're next!'

Anas Nur (12)
Beths Grammar School, Bexley

The Haunted Boat

Floating through the sea. 'Where we going, lads?'
'Captain, the boat's going to sink!'
The sea was blistering cold. It was dangerous. *Bang!* The boat
cracked open. The boat started flooding. Everyone was going to
drown. A weird-looking creature swept up into the boat. All stood
back. 'Bananas!' it shouted. It approached them ever so slowly,
dragging green, slimy seaweed with it. It pushed one of the workers
and he toppled overboard.
'What god-like strength does it have?' exclaimed a worker.
The gifted creature attacked everyone, leaving the captain. 'This was
my boat before he killed me.'

SULAIMAN KHOKHAR (11)
Beths Grammar School, Bexley

IT'S THERE BEHIND YOU

My feet clumped along the floor. I knew it was following me, I could feel it. Rain was hitting my face. I wondered if this was the last time I'd feel the rain. It was almost midnight. Oh no! I had limited time left. A flight of stairs seemed to pop out of nowhere. I was nearly there. The rain was getting worse. I knew it was right behind me. My house. I saw it, my safe haven. I ran to the door and frantically turned the handle, but it didn't turn. I heard breathing behind me. Then, I fainted...

FELIKS SCHEICH (12)
Beths Grammar School, Bexley

WORDS OF...

'Twas a cold night in his grandma's house. He was alone. The light in the hall flickered. The boy walked to the tap, it was dripping as usual, but the drip was not water, it was blood. He sprinted and locked himself in the room. Footsteps sounded, chasing him. Suddenly, it all went silent. The boy hid under the covers. A knock on the door. He didn't move. He denied this thing existed. The words came, he knew what this meant. Death. But what he didn't expect was how such spine-chilling words could be uttered.

SAMUEL WELLER
Beths Grammar School, Bexley

The Glasses Of Doom

He picked up his new prescription glasses. They fitted perfectly on his head. Darkness... Thomas Stones was now in a parallel universe, he just didn't know it yet. Nothing had changed for Tom, he was still admiring his new glasses in the mirror. He questioned in a heartwarming voice, 'What do you think, Mum, Dad?' As Tom turned around with an orange slice-shaped grin, it hit him. Bitter liquid dripped down his warm face. Where were Mum and Dad? Where were the humans? He removed the glasses... everything normal again.
'I think I'm OK, this time.'

SAM BAINES (12)
Beths Grammar School, Bexley

Daisy

I cautiously make my way towards the locked room where the noise that has been bothering me for the past hour is coming from. With each step I take, the noise becomes louder. With my heart in my mouth, I open the door, only to find myself face-to-face with my daughter's doll, Daisy. I could have sworn my daughter was holding her when she went to sleep. A dripping sound interrupts my thoughts. I did turn off the taps. Right? I sprint to my daughter's room, finding blood splattered everywhere and Daisy clutching a butcher's knife...

NABIL MOHAMED NUUR (12)
Beths Grammar School, Bexley

ARMAGEDDON

'Mike!' Dom called. 'We've got to get out of here!' Distant creatures lurked among the curious pair of boys who sought protection from a horrific amount of disgusting, revolting cranks who gorged on blood. 'Look, destroying everything is the only... '
Silence consumed the barren tunnel as Mike's voice had gone astray. 'Mike!'
Then, as Dom tried to find his friend, a dismembered, battered man appeared. Dom was paralysed with fear. He only said a few words, but they were enough to make your blood curdle. 'I give you five seconds to run away.'
Dom ran for his life.

BENJAMIN RICHARDS (12)
Beths Grammar School, Bexley

DETENTIONS

The building was engulfed in a thick mist. The wind whistled in the darkness. Factories puffed out fumes every minute on the cold Friday evening. No one was to be seen but a boy. The boy could vaguely see dancing but they were distorted. The boy stared at a page. It moved and slowly but surely it was getting closer. It flew into the ceiling, handle first, the floor had been washed in ceramic. The boy took no notice of it. Out of the cupboard burst a safe. Should he open it?

DHRUV RUDA (12)
Beths Grammar School, Bexley

The Blood Pen

Detention. Detention. Detention. The words going through Jack's head was one. His legs moved in the shape of the words in his head. The door was already open like it knew what Jack was here for. Entering with a grudge, there was a pen waiting for him. The moment it touched his hand, he felt like he was drugged. Detention. Detention. Detention. The word dripping from his head to the paper. The surge of pain going through his hand. A craving of the word 'detention'. He knew he was going to continue writing detention, detention, detention. The word of death.

ZAKARIYA HASSAN (12)
Beths Grammar School, Bexley

The Shadow

It was dark, the night crawled in. The fog thickened by the second. Katherine was walking home. She had suffered all day to find herself food. An alleyway back to her house was where no one went. The only thing to live there was death. When the clock struck 12am, anyone on the street would die. Katherine wasn't scared, she just ran and ran. *Ding!* The clock struck 12am. Immediately, Katherine felt weak. She fainted...
She woke up to find herself in a jail. All of a sudden, a pair of red eyes approached her quietly and extremely slowly...

NANA KWASI NORNOO (11)
Beths Grammar School, Bexley

DEADLY CHRISTMAS

The weather outside was horrible. It was a mixture of snow and rain. Jack knew it was going to be the worst Christmas ever. He lived in a flat with his parents. He was 12 years old.

Jack was about to go to sleep on Christmas Eve when suddenly, *shriek!* Footsteps could be heard on the landing. He started to panic. His cat shrieked, *miaow!* Then his door opened. He could see someone covered in blood. This person had a knife in his stomach. Jack's heart began to beat fast. This person was not just someone, it was his dad!

CHARLIE WILLIAMS (11)
Beths Grammar School, Bexley

THE HOUSE FROM HELL

Grey clouds engulfed the haunted house, plunging it into darkness. It was on top of a colossal steep hill. Leisurely, I meandered towards the dilapidated door covered in silhouetted cobwebs. The nefarious clouds ganged up on me, trying to strike me down like bullies. Paralysed with fear, I crept up the ancient staircase, shivering at every step.

Gingerly, I entered the house from hell. I heard something. What was it? A crow? It couldn't be. It was a scream. Another scream. 'Hello, anyone there?' Nothing. Another scream. What was it? I went upstairs, opened the door, and there was...

HENRY MCCUMESKY (11)
Beths Grammar School, Bexley

THE DOLL

The neglected cottage sat in the gloomy, remote darkness of the forest. The rusty gate creaked on its hinges. Tom froze. There, written with a bloody hand were the words: 'Leave'. Tom staggered before rushing into the cottage. His heart pounded in his chest as warm sweat trickled down his forehead. Just then, he saw them, dolls neatly lined up against the wall. He picked one up, which looked particularly like him, and plunged a sharp needle in its throat, but he knew he had made a mistake when he felt a pain. He clutched his throat...

HUGO CHANTELOUP (12)
Beths Grammar School, Bexley

WHAT LURKS THERE?

There he was in the forest all alone, little Tom with no one. No one to accompany him. The fog was closing in and he had to find shelter fast before it found him. Black Death. He had just found a deep cave when he thought to himself, *what lurks there?* But he fought his fear and went in. It was dark and gloomy in the cave. The shadows that were once small became big. The noises that were distant came closer, then a cold, clammy hand touched his shoulder and whispered, 'How much meat is on you?'

NOAH BEEBY-BROWN
Beths Grammar School, Bexley

WHO'S THERE?

I woke in the middle of the night to the creaking of my rusty, ancient, decrepit door. Trying to go back to sleep, I buried my head in my pillow. Then I realised that the curtains were open. I got out of bed and when my foot felt carpet, I heard a sound. I looked out of the window. 'Help us,' ringing in my ears. A gnome's lips moving!
I was panting, running to my dad's room. I put my hand on the door handle and felt hot breath on my back. 'Who's there?'

OSCAR LEO HARRIS (11)
Beths Grammar School, Bexley

THE ALIENS

2029. Hell broke loose, the aliens were here.
In the back of a car, sitting nervously on a great leather seat was a boy - fourteen years old. He had curly black hair and brave, intelligent eyes. Suddenly, a hard voice appeared on the radio.
'Jason, Jason Rich, tell your driver to pull up outside the dark, sharp military gates; or you'll never see your parents again.' Jason told his driver to do as requested.
When Jason arrived, his parents were on the floor with blood oozing out of their bodies...

JACOB CIRILLO (12)
Beths Grammar School, Bexley

The House With Deadly Eyes

'Did you see that?' gasped Ben.
'Yeah,' replied Musa.
'Those eyes... they just moved.'
'Just keep moving,' said Ben.
Suddenly, silence... then... cackling. Then the lights flickered on. A black figure appeared in the distance. Ben and Musa were tied up and were attempting to free themselves. A split-second later, a knife appeared and then there was nothing... just nothing. Ben and Musa were gone...

MICHAEL OLATUNJI-OJO (11)
Beths Grammar School, Bexley

It!

As I dock at this incantation of a metropolis, the elephantine establishments impose over me. A shadow shifts. Who is it? What is it? My heart skips a beat as I briskly move on. There it is again, and there, and there; how many are there? Is it an it, or is it a them? Now I'm running, running faster than I thought I could. I stumble. I know my life will end if it catches me, so I'm running again, faster, faster still. Oh God, it's fast, faster than me. *Bang!* I'm gone. If I'm dead, who's writing this?

KIRK POWELL (12)
Borden Grammar School, Sittingbourne

DON'T IGNORE ME!

A boy and his family are moving house. This new house was an abandoned house where a man had committed suicide. As soon as the family walked in their new house, they almost instantly regretted it. Their dog's head, hanging on the wall, one ear on, one ear hanging off. Silence came upon them, then a girl singing. They waited until the final word which didn't come. Instead a girl started screaming. Freaked out, the family panicked. All doors locked, no escape. *Bang!* The door got knocked down, a girl holding the dog's carcass said softly, 'Please don't ignore me.'

LUKE SCOTT-MORGAN (13)
Borden Grammar School, Sittingbourne

DEATH ON THE CLIFF

Steve was on a tall cliff and was looking at the wonderful view. 'This is amazing, I'm totally coming here again.'
Suddenly, behind him, a vampire appeared. He was very silent. His teeth came out like a rabbit. The vampire tiptoed towards Steve. Steve stood still, he had no idea what lurked behind him. A hand touched Steve's shoulder and the vampire spun Steve around. 'You'll never come here again,' said the vampire in his low, deep voice. With that said, he pushed Steve off the cliff. Steve fell with a high-pitched scream. The vampire walked away quietly.

BRADLEY ADKINS (12)
Borden Grammar School, Sittingbourne

On Halloween Night

Four teenagers, one spooky mansion, Halloween night. Doorbell pressed, the doors flung open. Ghosts appeared left and right! Grabbing all but one, ripping them limb from limb. The one left had a ghost costume. Pegging it out the back door, going head first into a water butt. It wobbled back and forth. Ghosts launched towards him! Falling back, toppling over the water butt. Spilling everywhere, the ghosts went up in puffs of smoke. Water was their weakness! Remembering a sword inside forged of deep stone, a rock from the sea's depths. An opportunity to escape? But would he make it?

SAM COLE (12)
Borden Grammar School, Sittingbourne

The Loft

There was a house. It was haunted. Yoshi slept in his room just like normal but every night he heard screams coming from the loft. When he went to check, blood dripped down from it. One day, he plucked up some courage to actually go into the loft. But when he did, he took a Magnum with him. When he got into the loft, he didn't hear any screams but he saw people getting sliced in half by a saw bug. When he saw it, he shot it but missed. The bug came towards him with its blade spinning viciously...

DECLAN APPS (12)
Borden Grammar School, Sittingbourne

VAMPIRE VICTIMS

As Gertrude walked into the Victorian house, she heard a loud scream. This sent a shiver down her spine as she knew there was a chance there were vampires hiding in the house.

She walked up the oak staircase, that made a really loud creak every time she gingerly inched up it. She saw the first signs of vampire life. There were bats staring at her like hawks. As she scanned her surroundings, on the landing she saw a message in blood: 'Carry on, you will be dead!' She screamed loudly! The sharp teeth pierced through...

FINLAY HARWOOD (12)
Borden Grammar School, Sittingbourne

DEAD!

I couldn't move my hand. It was wrapped around the handle of the gun, gripped tight, white knuckles flaring violently. The blood was everywhere; splattered across the walls to the ceiling, dripping from the overfilled tub, the woman inside limp, arm hanging lifelessly over the side. *Drip!* There was a hole in her head and parts of her brain floated in the crimson tide. I glanced at the mirror, sprayed red. The smile on my face had vanished, gone from existence, wiped off, dared me to move on. We had walked in together, separate, and walked out as one.

BENJAMIN BEARD (12)
Borden Grammar School, Sittingbourne

Iwanowanga

Once there was a crazy alien called Fib Bortuna. He was so mad that he went around killing people for fun. He strangled people to death with his tentacle on the side of his head. Whilst he was killing them, he shouted out, 'Iwanowanga' as his battle cry. After he had killed them, he would bite their heads off and mount them on the wall of his cave. If he ran out of room to mount heads, he would eat them and mount more in his dark, dank cave. Fib will always be lurking deep in the dark whispering, 'Iwanowanga'.

Joseph Bullock (12)
Borden Grammar School, Sittingbourne

The Thing

It was a dark, stormy night. The torches were blown out by the wind, the sky illuminated only by the full moon and the frequent flashes of lightning. There was an ordinary couple, or a couple that were ordinary any other night, but this night was different. This was the night they met The Thing. No one saw it and lived. Many doubted it existed, but why else were people disappearing? Why else were the dead, half-eaten bodies left at the graveyard? The couple were passing it when it happened... when the unfortunate couple met... The Thing.

Jack Cherrett (12)
Borden Grammar School, Sittingbourne

WHAT?

There he stood, almost paralysed. Fear rushed through his veins and he struggled to breathe. He pleaded not to be hurt, but the vicious man grabbed him by the collar and chucked him to the ground. He reached into his pocket and pulled out a razor-sharp blade that glistened in the light. He put it to the boy's throat and whispered, 'Where is it?' But he said nothing so the unrecognisable man asked the fearful boy again, but with an angrier tone. With one blow to the face, the man fell to the ground and the boy scrambled to safety.

MICHAEL KENT (12)
Borden Grammar School, Sittingbourne

REMEMBER ME?

I am running. Quicker than usual. It is my only chance of survival. I peer behind me, he is still there, still chasing, still smiling, still killing. I trip and fall onto the floor. I scream. It is no use. No one can help me. It is midnight and I have no other choices. I close my eyes and expect the worst, but instead, he says, 'Remember me?' He laughs. I open my eyes. How could I forget that clown mask? Before I can clock him properly, the knife pierces my neck. Goodbye cruel world. I am dead!

JOSHUA KURSZEWSKI (12)
Borden Grammar School, Sittingbourne

THERE IS NO ESCAPE

The party couldn't be better, people everywhere! The music is so loud, the speakers make the ground shake like mad! Until the speakers blow up, but the floor is still shaking. We hear a single man scream, 'Zombies!' In addition, the house gets smaller, squishing us together. The zombies are eating person to person and are getting squished by the walls closing in. There aren't many people left, about fifteen. The house is getting too small and the eaten people are turning! A zombie grabs my friend and eats him! I'm trapped, I accept it and close my eyes.

LUKE MATTHEW ALLEN (13)
Borden Grammar School, Sittingbourne

THE EVIL DOCTOR!

The spiky, sharp syringe entered the middle of his shaking arm. Crimson blood squirted all over the sea-blue curtains. Evilly, the doctor with crooked teeth and black, curly hair, glanced at the wound in his arm. The poor boy was petrified. He screamed, 'Patch it up! Patch it up!'
The evil doctor muttered, 'I'm here to do my job.'
She trampled over towards a pair of scissors, picked them up and locked the door. Then she lumbered back towards the little kid. She viciously shoved the scissors through his eye and the loudness of the scream was unreal. Dead!

RICCARDO DI CICCO (13)
Borden Grammar School, Sittingbourne

THE GRAVEYARD

One night, I was strolling past the graveyard to get home and in a flash, bodies came to life, all of the dead bodies rose in their form... zombies! Ankles torn to shreds, all limbs broken and skin as rancid as dead meat. They were chasing me, which meant I was running for survival, they were screeching, 'You will die tonight, there's no one left to call for help!' I ran home as quickly as I could and found out something dreadful... my family were part of the zombie apocalypse and I witnessed where they were going... the graveyard!

HARRISON JAMES (12)
Borden Grammar School, Sittingbourne

THE MAN IN THE CORNER

Another one gone. Another one dead. Another one he had killed. Why? Because he found it fun. Now it was time to go to bed. In bed, nice and cosy. Turns to the corner for no particular reason. A man. A man is in the corner. Just standing there. But not any man. The one he killed. No, it can't be. Impossible. The murderer rubs his eyes. The man's one step closer. The murderer blinks. One step closer. The murderer tries not to blink but can't help it. One step. He's an inch from him. The murderer blinks. He dies.

MATTHEW REEVES (13)
Borden Grammar School, Sittingbourne

DEAD

He dropped. Lying on his side. Dead. A hole already dug. Flowers already prepared. Someone, or perhaps something, had known he'd be here tonight, meeting his death. He was tough, but not tough enough for here. Especially at night, with only the moonlight and instincts guiding you along the bumpy, cold stone path. Groups of men, mostly ex-army, had entered before seeking the truth or even sometimes revenge. Only a few had ever returned, but eventually died from injuries. He had no idea of what he had let himself in for and wouldn't be able to tell his horrific tale.

SAM CROSS (13)
Borden Grammar School, Sittingbourne

THE GIRL WHO WAS FOUND

The wooden panels creaked under my feet. At first, I thought I was alone. Then something, someone moved. I pushed on the first bedroom door I came to. It swung open. I felt I was transported back to... my house? My room? From the dusty, mysterious corridors came this surprise, my heart slowed. Crouching, I inspected the immaculately made covers before me. I uttered the words, 'Is this mine?' At this surprise, I forgot my search for... her. A shock passed through my spine and I fell limp to the bed. She stood in the doorway, staring into my soul.

JAKE BURNS (12)
Borden Grammar School, Sittingbourne

The New House

I reached for my flashlight. I turn it on, it flickers away in the piercing moonlight shining from the splintered wooden-framed window. I meander downstairs to replace the batteries. I see a glowing in the kitchen... I'm frozen in fear as the cold, perished body of my mother lies on the hard granite floor. Blood squirting out of a vein in her neck, it has been slit, deep. I hear dripping behind me. I turn. It lunges a knife in the back of my neck. I feel it pierce out the other side of my neck. Then it grins...

Thomas Watson (12)
Borden Grammar School, Sittingbourne

The Creepy Graveyard

He silently crept into the graveyard, peering through the gloom of dawn but could only just make out the exit which appeared further away with every step he took. The crack of branches under his feet and blood pounding in his ears were the only sounds breaking the eerie silence. He stumbled on the uneven ground and instinctively reached out to break his fall. To his horror, he realised the grave was open! In his daze he saw a decaying hand with bones sticking out drawing nearer. The air stank of rotting flesh as he fell into unconsciousness...

Campbell Horton (12)
Borden Grammar School, Sittingbourne

Suffocation

I fall, the wind taking my breath away. The dark, foggy trees cover the sky, plunging me into darkness. The sheer collision into the water was enough for my blood to stain the lake. I open my mouth, hoping for oxygen. Being in an atmosphere surrounded by dark, deathly trees and shrubs is an experience in itself. Water floods my mouth. I swallow the mossy water, choking my lungs, coughing blood up. My heart travels from my body, taking my breath with it. My heart sinks down the lake. My life flashes before me. It's here. The end is here.

Archie Bodiam (12)
Borden Grammar School, Sittingbourne

Daisy And Her Lamp

It was 2am when the scream echoed around the house. It wasn't just a normal, playful scream, this was a blood-curdling shriek, full of pure and utter terror.
Daisy woke abruptly. Her innocent dreams had been shattered by a strange noise. It sounded like a scream to her. She was curious so she turned on her lamp. Her dolls formed eerie shadows. Daisy heard footsteps out in the corridor. 'Mum?' she whispered. More footsteps. 'Mummy? What is it, Mummy?' Daisy then felt cold, alone, so cold. The door handle turned slowly, the door creaking open... and her lamp... went... out...

Jacob Fletcher (12)
Borden Grammar School, Sittingbourne

The Graveyard

On a dark and gloomy night, the graveyard stood still as a raging storm towered over the city of London. A girl, no bigger than you and I, strolled into the unknown. The atmosphere was quiet as the girl nervously stuttered to a grave. The grave said, 'All shall die'. The anxious girl turned to see a boy slowly walking towards her. 'Ah,' the girl said, 'I'm glad to see you.'
The boy said nothing. He stood there motionless, staring at the girl. The girl tiptoed to the boy, wondering if he would move, but that's when he *pounced...*

Flynn Toon (13)
Borden Grammar School, Sittingbourne

Shadow Creeper

Razz's fate was determined the day his father was killed. Ghosts don't murder, they haunt. They instil fear. They might inhabit someone's mind and drive them to suicide, but actual slaughter is rare. Razz's father was murdered by a ghost. On that day Razz became a ghost hunter. He inhabited the darkness. He learned about betrayal, lonely hearts and the isolation of eternity. He drank the whispers and sang misfortune. He became a lost soul. It was upon his death, he knew he would become a ghost and see his father in the deathly shadows.

Ryan Lewis (13)
Borden Grammar School, Sittingbourne

THAT ONE NIGHT

It was the one night I wasn't afraid. I was out trick or treating on my estate. It was all laughing and scaring each other until *he* stood in front of me and my friends. There was nobody else around. The mysterious person had a freaky orange pumpkin mask. *He* said that during the next three days all we would see was him. He would know where we were and what we would be doing. After three days he would kill us and our families...

DANIEL LATHAM (12)
Borden Grammar School, Sittingbourne

THE RUN

It was the dead of night. Mist was creeping around the looming tombstones like icy fingers trying to grab me. There was a shuffle in the dark. I ran inside the old church looking for some kind of life or refuge. But inside, there was no one, just blackness. I walked in warily, my head darting side to side. I sat down on the icy-cold pew... and the door creaked open. I released the breath I'd been holding subconsciously. A hand grabbed my arm and pulled me backwards. I shrieked and screamed as I was pulled into the air...

LUKE STRINGER
Borden Grammar School, Sittingbourne

THE VOID

Round and round I go, spinning in the void. I don't know where I'm going in the tunnel of darkness, but I know I'm feeling dizzy and can hear screaming; a scream like a little girl heading towards death. My mind has gone crazy. I think I'm hypnotised. I'm still spinning, round and round I go, spinning in the void. Suddenly, it goes eerie. I can hear an evil laugh. My heart's thumping like a drum. I hear a woman talking to me. 'Goodnight my dear, as these are your final seconds.' The entire world around me goes completely silent...

OSCAR PATTERN (12)
Borden Grammar School, Sittingbourne

GONE

As the misty air sets, so does the sun. I'm stranded here alone. The remaining fog rolls effortlessly over the laces of my shoes. Where is she? She's gone. A flash, a bang and she's gone. I'm frozen with fear, not knowing what to do. All the birds fall silent as a loud crack pierces into the atmosphere. Then I see it, a shack. The trees of the forest will not stand in my way. I'm at the foot of the shack and then I hear them. The stamping of feet, coming straight for me. I freeze. Jane?

ZACHARY SMITH (13)
Borden Grammar School, Sittingbourne

Lost In The Mist

Ruth was walking through the woods alone. It was a dark and gloomy night. She only had one thing on her mind, to find her brother. She heard the little lullaby before he was gone. Ruth kept trekking in the woods to find him, trying not to make a single sound. However, she felt a shiver down her spine, she knew she was not alone. This was enough to make her run and whatever she heard was after her too. Suddenly, when she thought she was clear... she heard the little lullaby... before she was taken away.

CHIMELAM IGWE (13)
Borden Grammar School, Sittingbourne

Zack The Snipper

It was a chilly night. Hannah ran. When she arrived at the salon, the lights were off. She knocked. The oak door creaked open. 'Hello,' she said, a tremor in her voice. 'Is anyone there?' No reply. Suddenly, an icy hand pushed her inside. She turned, but nobody was there. 'Who are you?' she whispered, her face sodden with tears. The door slammed. Green eyes flashed. Hannah flicked her torch on with trembling hands. In cold torchlight, a black cat slithered onto a chair. A mirror smashed. Hannah's body shook as she shrieked, 'Where's my hairdresser?'

ED HOLMES (12)
Borden Grammar School, Sittingbourne

THE MIDNIGHT MURDERER

It was Halloween night. Jamie was walking through the woods in silence. All of a sudden, a blood-curdling scream pierced the mist. Jamie investigated what the source of the noise was. He was trekking through the mist when he saw something move behind a tree. He then realised it was his best friend, Michael. When they finally went to bed, the scream was still in his head. At midnight, Michael got out of his bed and slit Jamie's throat while he slept. Jamie let out an agonised scream and, as he fell, he saw a decaying body on the floor.

JAMIE KING (12)
Borden Grammar School, Sittingbourne

THE CRATE

I pull out my pistol in my right hand, flashlight in my left and cross it over my gun. It was unlocked when it was found. Lock broken, door slightly open. Walking in, I find: arms, legs, bones and heads with holes in the necks of them. I have never seen anything like this in my time! This is hopefully the worst thing I will ever see in my life! I wonder if it was a sabretooth or something. I decide to go further in. However, before I can make it two more steps, I hear a growl echo...

PETER HENDRY (12)
Borden Grammar School, Sittingbourne

The Game

'Are you afraid?' David asked curiously.

The two brothers, David and Jonathon, were about to play a game that had haunted the town for many generations. It was called 'The Charlie Charlie game'. It called a spirit to do things unknown to society.

'Charlie, Charlie, are you there?' The brothers repeated it again.

'Charlie, Charlie, are you there?'

Suddenly, the glass in the hose broke but in a split second, Jonathon saw a shadowy figure and as soon as he was going to say something, a knife went straight through both of them like a boomerang!

Tyresse Bundu-Kamara (12)
Borden Grammar School, Sittingbourne

THE SHOP SCARE

Ring, ring! Ring, ring! My phone rang. It was Toby. 'Meet me at the sweet shop,' Toby stated, but it wasn't Toby's voice. It was deeper, more rusty than Toby's. I ended the call.

When I got to the sweet shop, no one was there, but there was a shadow, one I hadn't seen before. I peered round the dark, gloomy corner, only to find an abandoned, skinny cat trying to clean her kittens. I turned back around and tried to open the creaky shop door. It was unlocked. I heard noises from the back room. I saw a shadow...

OLLY STURROCK-LEATON (12)
Borden Grammar School, Sittingbourne

DREAMLAND

Bang! A loud sound woke me up. I looked around to see if it was the wind, but it wasn't. I slowly got up and opened the door. It creaked loudly and a shiver went down my spine. I could hear whispering now and footsteps slowly getting louder and closer. I was frozen, unable to think of what to do. It was really loud now and before I knew it, a hooded figure appeared in front.

'No, get away!'

I jumped out of bed, puffing for breath. 'Oh, it was just a dream!' But then I heard a loud bang...

HARIS KHAN (13)
Borden Grammar School, Sittingbourne

THE CASTLE

It was a cold November night and Paul and Matt decided to trek up to the spooky castle on top of the hill. Little did they know it was haunted. It's a long walk to the castle but they got there in the end. They walked inside cautiously. Matt walked ahead while Paul stayed behind. Suddenly, they heard something. It was... the castle's demon. It started chasing them. They had nowhere to run, nowhere to hide. They eventually ran outside for their lives, but only Paul made it...

CHARLIE O'REILLY (13)
Borden Grammar School, Sittingbourne

THE SOBBING

I woke abruptly from my sleep. It was exactly midnight. There was no wind or noise so I wondered how I woke up. Just as I was about to fall back to sleep, I heard a muffled sobbing sound coming from my bathroom. Curious, I got out of bed, grabbed my torch and gingerly walked over. I thought I saw something on the wall but when I shone the torch over it, there was nothing. The sobbing was getting louder, so was my heart in my ears. Legs like jelly. Opened door. Torch flickered off. Heart stopped... there it was.

TOBY HEATHER (13)
Borden Grammar School, Sittingbourne

THE FAMILY REUNION

It was the day of the family reunion. I was extremely excited. It came to 5pm and it was time to start getting ready. I started to put my smart clothes on to dress for the occasion. I heard a smash of glass and looked straight at the window. Nothing had changed. At this point I was freaking out. Being alone is scary enough at night, let alone this paranormal activity. I went to the next glass object in my room. I stared in the mirror when my reflection suddenly smiled. I turned and was confronted by endless darkness...

RORY KIMBER (12)
Borden Grammar School, Sittingbourne

THE PSYCHOPATH

I ran, I couldn't stop otherwise he would grab me. I needed a plan, quickly. I started climbing a tree but the psychopath dragged me down. He tried to stab me with his razor-sharp knife. I rolled out the way. I shot up. I started running. I wasn't looking and I dropped down a steep hill and hit a tree. I thought I had got away but he looked straight into my eyes. I stumbled up, ran behind a tree, climbed up it. I dropped a knife into the top of his head. Blood went everywhere. He was dead.

MAC RICHARDSON (12)
Borden Grammar School, Sittingbourne

Shadows

Gore trickled from my lifeless corpse. Darkness stood opposite me. I glared down without any intention of doing so, to find a wound deep enough to cause excruciating pain to the other side of my now extinct body. The knees I used to amble with, now a piece of futile flesh, fell to the rigid ground. Without knowing, I was praying to God to indicate this wasn't real but just a nightmare. But of course, sinners don't get what they desire. Radiance assaulted the nearby earth to revile the shadow's face and with my last breath I whispered... 'Father.'

ADAM SELLINGS (12)
Borden Grammar School, Sittingbourne

Sleep Tight

There it was again, but this time it was underneath my bed! My heart pumped fear through my blood. I could see my own breath but it wasn't cold. I couldn't move. Fear pinned me to my sheets. Holding my duvet tightly to my chin with only my eyes visible, a dark, figureless silhouette stirred beneath my bed. I tried to resist the force pulling my duvet from my hands. Whilst petrified, I was compelled to take a glance. A bony, scaly hand with long, sharp nails was slowly gathering my duvet into its bloodthirsty mouth. Was I next?

GREGOR MCALLAN (12)
Borden Grammar School, Sittingbourne

ACTIONS

I'm running and running, faster than I've ever run before. I could sense his presence looming over me, his breath running down my spine. My chances of escape were now futile. I collapsed, giving in and waiting for the inevitable. Nothing. Silence. The sound of silence screamed louder than I could. I took a quick glimpse at nothing but the blackened forest. I let out a sigh of relief, slowly turning my head back around... there he was. His tall, hefty figure frightened me to the bone. I knew my actions would catch up with me, but not this soon...

GLORY KENUBIA (12)
Borden Grammar School, Sittingbourne

DEAD WOMAN'S TOUCH

I was strolling slowly down the street, my footsteps an echo in the wind. I thought I could see my wife, my dead wife, my Sarah. She was in her wedding dress, blue, black and white. She had been dead for years now, I couldn't remember, maybe three years? I got closer and closer. I eventually got close and put my hand through the disappearing mist of her. I felt a hand on my shoulder. As I put my hand on it, it was cold. I was puzzled. I turned, saw something there and felt a hand go through me...

JAMIE MORROW (12)
Borden Grammar School, Sittingbourne

Diseased Miner

Unfortunately, on the day I started my new job, going down into the mine, I had the feeling that something bad was going to happen. In the mine, blackness smeared, filled and pulled my heart apart, crunching my organs with every step I took. Rapidly gagging on blood, my hollow echo was not clear enough for anyone to hear. Not a single soul came to help. The elevator tormented me, stopping me escaping my hell. This was the end.
Suddenly, a shadow emerged before my eyes. 'Thank God, I'll be saved.' Nope, it was a rat, ready for dinner!

ALEX GREEN (12)
Borden Grammar School, Sittingbourne

An Uninvited Guest

The frantic jerking of the door was what woke me. The door creaked open revealing a malevolent form, hair shrouding its face, standing in the doorway. The creature stumbled slowly across the dark room. Looming over my bed, she reached behind her back. Wildly looking around the room, my eyes found the clock. Through the darkness I managed to make out 2:07am. Her arm began to reappear. I screamed and awoke. It must have been a dream.
I look up at the clock. It is 2:06am. I hear footsteps coming up the stairs, but no one's home...

CONNOR ROSEWELL (14)
Goldwyn Plus, Ashford

SHADOW

The rustling in the bush was terrifying. As I sped up, I gradually started a gentle jog. Something was in that bush. All I could think about was getting away, but how?

Every noise I heard, I jumped. Paranoia kicked in. I could hear the sound of my own heartbeat. Only five minutes away from home and the noise started again, only getting louder and louder.

Bang! I was home, the door was locked and I felt safer. Walking over to shut my curtains, a shadow passed the window. I looked out but nothing was there.

Knock, knock, knock!

ABBIE SPENCER (15)
Goldwyn Plus, Ashford

THE SILHOUETTE

I crept down the dingy hallway and paused by the front door. The knocker outside hammered against the door. I backed away. The fog, which had settled against the frosted window, lingered a moment then unveiled a shadowy silhouette. Long, crippled fingers tapped against the window. I fled. I slipped and crashed to the floor.

When I eventually came to, I was light-headed. I got up with the assistance of a chest of drawers and peered around. To my horror, I saw the front door blowing open in the wind. Whatever was outside was now very much in...

EMILY BENNEY (15)
High Weald Academy, Cranbrook

AMNESIA

The pain was excruciating. Coughing, blood spilled over my lips. My lungs burned. A sensation similar to amnesia swept over me. Why was I here? Who was I? I felt nauseous. Limbs aching, I tried to move. Harsh, broken light glared above, covered in maggots and decaying rust. Terrified, I yelped as I realised there was a cut above my right brow. I woke up. The room was cold. The nightmare over. My lungs began to burn. I tried to move. It wasn't a dream...

KIAYA ROSE STORM BAILEY (14)
High Weald Academy, Cranbrook

IN THE DARK

It was a bleak, dreary night as the couple drove through the menacing trees. The radio blared a heavy beat that was interrupted by something appearing in the dying headlights. A loud *thud* followed. Cursing under his breath, the man braked harshly and almost leapt out of his car to inspect the bumper. Once satisfied of his car's wellbeing, he strode round the back of the car, out of the light. His wife then heard a sickening crunch, followed by a thud. The now widow let out a small scream as her door opened...
The police arrived much later...

WILLIAM BUSHNELL (14)
High Weald Academy, Cranbrook

THE ALLEYWAY

The alleyway is too quiet. The lights are off. I begin walking, when I suddenly stop. I hear a cry; I turn around to see a girl holding a doll. It has a severed arm and torn clothes. I ask the girl if she is okay. It is hard to see, but she looks the same as the doll she is holding, only, she is bleeding from her eyes.
A demonic voice says, 'Run!' I'm running and I trip. I have been impaled on a rusty dagger.
She is laughing.
If you read this, there is no escape.

JOEL BLACK (12)
Langley Park School for Boys, Beckenham

BOO BOO BLACK SHEEP

'Boo Boo black sheep, have you any wool?'
Boo Boo Black Sheep was Baa Baa's cousin. He was not as cute as Baa Baa Black Sheep. Every night, instead of heading back to the barn, he would wander off into the night and use his razor-sharp nails to kill anything near him.
On Christmas Eve, Boo Boo heard sleigh bells ringing high up above. Looking up to the sky, he saw a sleigh flying. Sharpening his nails, Boo Boo flew up into the night sky and dug his claws into Santa Claus' heart.

SCOTT STOREY (11)
Langley Park School for Boys, Beckenham

The Shadow

The parents told the boy they'd be back at midnight. As he heard the door slam shut, he waited.

As he lay wrapped in his thick duvet, he heard a smash downstairs. An echoing voice whispered to him, but he could not decipher what it was saying. He heard the shadows creak and an unwelcome shiver trickled down his spine. Then the shadow, the haunting shadow, seeped through the door. In its hand rested a curved blade, lined in blood. The shadow lingered, slowly coming towards him and shoved the knife through his chest.

The boy dropped dead.

ALEX HAMILTON
Langley Park School for Boys, Beckenham

Dilemma

A cold winter night in the isolated suburbs of West England. Nothing stirred in the night but mysterious murmurs came from downstairs. Startled, yet intrigued, I glided out onto the landing. Downstairs, all that I heard was the deafening whispers of my mother. I'd never heard her so despairing and before I could descend further, a figure stood in the corner of the room to my left. It was my mother. The words she spoke sent shivers from head to toe. A painful embrace that shook each nerve. 'Don't go downstairs, I heard it too. That... is not your mother.'

TOM CRAWFORD (17)
St George's CE School, Gravesend

AXE

Slowly, the young woman stumbled down the hallway, blood dripping onto the wooden floor from her fingers. Every so often she would slip slightly on the deep red puddles that she seemed to be following, barely finding her footing in the interval between each. Yet she continued. Passing one door on the left, then another on the right. As she continued down the corridor, a doorway came into view that caused a deathly sparkle to appear in her eyes. Gripping the axe tighter, without so much as a glance over her shoulder, she entered...

LEAH HOCKLEY (17)
St George's CE School, Gravesend

HIS WHISPER

The lights flickered. Annalise looked at her reflection. The rip in her gown revealed the gash on her leg. Blood. Seeping slowly in the satin. She ran. The echoes of footsteps behind her. Stopping, she found herself there, where she vowed never to set foot again. The wind screamed outside. Water leaked from the ceiling onto the marble floor. *Tap, tap, tap.* The smell of lilies invaded her nostrils. Beads of sweat rolled down her forehead. Palms clammy. She shuddered as someone's breath tickled her neck. Hands gripped her waist! Covered her mouth! His whisper filled the room.
'Gotcha!'

RAMINA BENNING (17)
St George's CE School, Gravesend

Untitled

Alone, coldness intertwined in the wind, breathing, slithering around me. I'm watching. Listening. Lurking. The trees are whispering and so am I. I'm good at hiding, at least you've never seen me. You don't even know I exist. But, technically I don't really. Do I? I just want to be your friend. Take you to my favourite place. But, my last friend didn't like it there. You might though. I thrive on your presence, it helps me survive. You're opening your window now. I guess I'm coming in. I'm not as scary as I look. Now, come play with me...

CHARLOTTE UONG (14)
St George's CE School, Gravesend

Blame

You blame the creaks on the stairs. You blame the whispers on the wind. You blame the mice for the scurrying sounds in the attic. You blame the tapping on the window on the trees. You think your mum called your name. You blame the flicker of the lights on faulty electricity. You blame the door swaying on the wind. You blame the steps late at night on your parents. You blame the shadows outside your window on the car lights. You blame the unearthly figures in the darkness on your mind, but maybe, just maybe they're me...

MEGAN BOTLEY (14)
St George's CE School, Gravesend

Reflection

I've been here a while... you have no idea do you? Never bothered to second guess why your window or wardrobe were open when you swear you shut it. I've been here waiting... it's nice watching you sleep, then wake releasing ear-piercing screams from your throat when you thought you heard a noise... never thought it was me, did you? I can hear you now... found my present yet? Hmm, Christmas dinner, nice isn't it? It won't last long. You should remember me by now, I mean... you don't look in the mirror for nothing.

Rebecca Elizabeth Bibby (15)
St George's CE School, Gravesend

Awoken

The silence was deafening. It echoed around the room like chattering whispers. My eye opened; engulfed by sheets. A sudden chill trailed down my shivering spine. Noises filled the air. Suddenly, chatters tiptoed silently up the stairs and into the dusky room. The whole room jolted. My stomach was like a bottomless pit, churning at every sound. *Creak!* The door slowly opened, releasing a beacon of light. I closed my eyes, hoping to drift asleep.
My heavy breathing was drowned by the noise of my phone, awakening me. The text read: 'I'm watching you, I'm watching you right now'.

Katie Taylor (14)
St George's CE School, Gravesend

THE ANIMAL

Oh god, the pain, I can feel its teeth ripping into my flesh. Its claws clamped tight on my leg like a vice. The smell of my own blood. I can feel the blood pulsing into my mouth, tasting like metal. My ears pounding with the beating of my heart that feels like it's going to burst like a balloon. I can't get free. Kicking it, hitting it, shouting, screaming. No one's coming to help. Is there no one left? So much blood and flesh everywhere. As I look down, I can slowly see myself being pulled into the darkness...

RUTH TAYLOR (14)
St George's CE School, Gravesend

ISLAND OF THE DOLLS

The derelict shack stood before me, clad with abandoned dolls; some severed, some broken, some with missing limbs. All I heard was the deafening silence of the forest. I felt as if they were watching me. Their eyes flicked on me. *Thud!* I had a spine-chilling feeling as the door opened with a piercing creak. *Who opened the door? Do I go in?*
As I walked in, there was nothing but uncomfortable darkness. *Drip!* I tore open the curtains. *Drip!* Dolls lay about the floor, all looking at something. I looked up. There it was...

DANIELLE RAYFIELD (14)
St George's CE School, Gravesend

SILENCE OF THE STORM

Cold steps crushing the blades growing along the soil below her, the plants tried to crawl up to her broken skin as she tried to escape. Cursed, that's what he was. Trapped in the dark abyss inside his head. Isolated, trapped, inside an abandoned hole in the earth, ivy-clad and crumbling towards the ground. His screech of frustration pierced the silence, shooting straight through her pounding heart. The trees had caught him. A blood-curdling scream emitting from behind her as nature fell silent. Tears of blood stained his tired face as everything stopped. Deafening silence tainted the air.

MIA REKERT (14)
St George's CE School, Gravesend

LOST IN THE UNKNOWN

My heart was pounding with fear. The screaming. The yelling. Death was calling through the moving woods. It touched me! But it was nothing. A sigh of relief shot through me. It touched me again! Why couldn't I see it? Where was it? Who was it? But there was no voice with a reply. I tried calling Folly. There was no answer, I heard a whisper of a girl speaking out. I couldn't understand her but it sounded like Folly, but she was nowhere to be seen. Was this the end for me?

KAROLINA SADOVSKA (15)
St George's CE School, Gravesend

THE OTHER REFLECTION

As I was transported back to reality, my eyes flitted open. I sat up slowly, being cautious with my head. For some reason it was pounding. I looked around. I was in a desolate, run-down house, the perfect hideout for a serial killer. There were holes in the roof, dust covering everything and rotten wood with dark spots as if someone had painted irregular polka dots. There was only one surface in the room that wasn't covered in dust. A mirror. I cautiously approached it. I saw myself in the mirror... and another reflection... I turned around to see the...

SOPHIE EHLES (15)
St George's CE School, Gravesend

THE GROWL

I was working at my desk in my living room with the baby monitor next to me. I was tired. She was finally sound asleep. I was nearly finished when I heard rustling from her room. Anxious, I looked at the CCTV in her room to see our dog growling at a black figure clutching my baby. I rubbed my eyes and glanced to see it staring right at me. The growling stopped in her room. It began to start growling again behind me and I heard the footsteps... one... two... three...

LIBBY BOROWCZYK (14)
St George's CE School, Gravesend

THE GLOVED HAND

Isolated...
As I turned I heard a scream. Then nothing. The culprit hushed abruptly. Nothing. Once again, the silence stabbed by an ear-piercing scream. I ran...
Whatever was out there was after me. Faster... the only sounds left were the thudding of my feet and the twigs behind me. Then I saw something. I stopped. The only sound to be heard was my heavy breathing. Then a branch snapped. I turned... nothing was behind me. I felt a hand on my shoulder pull me back. I went to scream but a gloved hand stopped all sound...

ELLEN ALDERSON (14)
St George's CE School, Gravesend

FOLLOWED

Crunch! Snap! Crunch! The echo of my footsteps burrowing like maggots into saturated soil resounded in my craze-infested mind. Eerie darkness consumed me in its isolating grip and shadowed the little moonlight my eyes fixated on desperately. If I hadn't heard the slightly mis-timed footfall, I would have said I was alone. However, the sense of being watched and the warm breath, only ghosting the back of my neck, told me otherwise. How did my own morbid infatuation for that shot of adrenaline coursing through my veins lead to my demise? I screamed. Then silence severed the forest.

KATHRYN MAIR (14)
St George's CE School, Gravesend

100 Missed Calls

My phone had been going all day. That wasn't unusual, but this phone was broken. A voice echoed through the isolated forest. '99 missed calls, one more to go.' I shivered and stared at the blank screen. Horrified. '100 missed.' I smashed the phone on the ground as the deafening silence was sliced by a blood-curdling scream. I looked up and it said, 'I warned you,' followed by deep breathing on my neck. The voice was deeper this time round. Hearing the urgency, I turned around, startled to see myself as the shadow took away my corpse.

Joy Ogunsola (14)
St George's CE School, Gravesend

Alone

'Argh!' The scream howled through the moonless night. Phantoms hovered through the pitchy night. The terrifying look at the crow's eyes sent ice-spikes down my spine. There I stood, deserted, in an intimidating corpse-like field. The frozen trees crackled like the wicked witch. There I was, standing waiting, waiting for something, something that never came. Then I saw something crawling towards me, something big, something angry. As it got closer and closer and closer, suddenly... something mysteriously grabbed out at me. Oh, the horror, oh the horror...
As I woke up from my sleep.

Oluwatobiloba Oluwaseun Kukoyi (15)
St George's CE School, Gravesend

THE BREAKDOWN

The car stopped and the only thing in the surroundings of the car was the creepy bed and breakfast. I knocked on the door but nobody answered. I slowly opened it. It creaked as it opened. I stepped inside. The place seemed abandoned. I called the car service. 'We will be there in 10 minutes.'
They'd better be, I thought to myself.
I heard someone scream from upstairs. I ran as fast as I could until I was dragged backwards. I screamed. As I started to turn around, it went silent. I was still in my car driving...

RUBY VERHAEREN (14)
St George's CE School, Gravesend

WHICH WAY?

I bolted through the forest. The wind smacked me dead in the face as I ran. It felt like a thunderstorm was brewing. I was determined to get to the other side. This eerie place was pitch-black with branches leaning in from every corner you could think of. They invaded your mind too. I began to believe there was no way out. All my instincts kicked in, pointing in different directions to sprint down. All this tension developed, getting to a higher level each second. I decided to agree with my gut.
A figure appeared in front of me...

SAMUEL LITHCO (15)
St George's CE School, Gravesend

Van Helsing's Children

Darkness clung to me, my lamplight quivering. I could sense I wasn't alone, for the air seemed too alive not to be. Eerily, I stepped forward. *Boom!* Flames ignited everywhere. I reared back, a great hall engulfing me. From the ceiling hung hundreds, if not thousands, of teeming, squirming, embriotic masses. Van Helsing's children. Sucking in the now stale air, I moved into the deadly incubator. What was that? A clawed hand burst from the ceiling, reaching out. Then another, and another. I was surrounded by the cruel undead and soon would join the bones beneath my cold feet.

SARAH CHAWNER (17)
St George's CE School, Gravesend

Untitled

As I awoke, I remembered nothing, not even my name. I'm in a house, there's blood leading to the hallway. It's the only way out, not that I want to go out. The door opens with a groan, the bloodstain leads into one of the other doors. I make the decision to open the door without blood beneath it. As it opens, I fall to the ground and bats fly out. I feel relieved, but then I see it. It stares directly at me, blood dripping off its teeth. That's all I remember.

RYAN WOODHOUSE (14)
St George's CE School, Gravesend

DEATH'S CHILDREN!

Once upon a time, there was a village on the outskirts of Mount Everest. Every night a child would go missing...

One day, the villagers decided to set a trap for the being that was abducting the innocent children. In the making of this trap, suddenly a bizarre howl was heard miles away, so loud it nearly burst the villagers' eardrums! The gallant man waited for the supernatural force. Suddenly, a malevolent being burst out of the forest, crushing everyone in its wake. *Bite, bite, bite!* Everyone was dead, there was no life to defeat this evil being.

AHMED AKBAR (14)
St George's CE School, Gravesend

THE FOREST OF DEATH!

A dark, gloomy forest of death, no birds singing, no animals about. Where was life?

I heard footsteps behind me, groaning and moaning, louder and louder. Halloween night at 1am. Suddenly, a glimpse of what looked like a zombie. Running. Faster and faster, something grabbed my arm, gnawing at my arm! I fell! My arm went numb. I could see street lights. Almost home. Running. I was home. I looked in the mirror and my arm was hanging on by a thread! What happened? Suddenly, I saw the same zombie at my window. Terrified, I threw myself under the bed...

LOUISE OUSLEY (15)
St George's CE School, Gravesend

HIDE-AND-SEEK!

Ba-dum. I could feel my heart beating like a drum, counting down my death. The only thing that stood between me and my freedom was a forest, dark as night. Ba-dum. I made my way down a gravel path. I heard a little girl sing, 'Ding-dong, here I come to find you. Hurry up and run. Let's play a little game and have fun.'
I sprinted. I slammed into something. I would have hurt my legs, but they were slowly being devoured by a creature never seen before. A blood-curdling scream was ripped from my throat...
'Found you!'

TAUNI BAXTER (15)
St George's CE School, Gravesend

UNTITLED

Halloween. One couple woke during the night. Crashes and bangs were heard in the caravan. Who was it? Where was it coming from? No one knew... He got up slowly to light the candles. He returned to bed and the candles blew out. He lit them again. They extinguished again. She screamed, 'Someone touched my leg!'
He shouted, 'Be quiet!' He heard eerie noises coming from the cupboard. Glasses were shaking and falling off the side like someone was pushing them off. He got up and the noises disappeared. He warily opened the door. Lurking. Waiting. Lightning struck!

CHLOE TURNER (14)
St George's CE School, Gravesend

THE MYSTERIOUS DISAPPEARANCE OF CHLOE

It was the night of Halloween, Chloe and I were on our way home from a party. A forest, dark, my heart was pounding. I said to Chloe, 'This is the only way home.'
We took a deep breath and decided to walk through the forest. As we walked and talked a strange noise was heard behind us. We decided to walk faster, but the noise would get closer. We decided to run. I could feel heavy breathing on my neck. I ran faster. As I came out of the forest, I turned and noticed Chloe was gone...

MARNIE TAYLOR (14)
St George's CE School, Gravesend

THE HOUSE, THE ROCKING CHAIR, A LITTLE GIRL... AND... RYLEIGH

Tayluer and I walked down the Yorkshire country lanes. Me, her. Alone. In the middle of the night. Not a light, not a sound. I shivered. An old house stood in front of us. We approached the ancient wooden door. *Creak!* The door flung open. Our hearts pounded. A rocking chair moving on its own. I screamed. A voice of a young girl spoke out. 'Why are you in my house?'
Tayluer panicked. 'It was Ryleigh's idea!'
I tried to run. I couldn't. Tayluer... gone! Me, alone, with the girl! I was going to be here forever, wasn't I?

CHLOE BROWN (15)
St George's CE School, Gravesend

Death Alley...

It was a dark night, covered by graves. The ghostly tension built in my veins. Fear ran through my bones. My hairs stuck up. The clouds were low and it made the night gloomy. I stepped forward, walking further, further and further. I forced myself to walk more, more and more. A force shoved me. My blood ran faster, heart pumped so fast. It was like something controlling my ghostly body. The graveyard lit up so bright, stroking me back a few steps. Suddenly, I blinked and a flash appeared, followed by the man himself. I couldn't believe my eyes...

Ollie Milioto (14)
St George's CE School, Gravesend

The Shadow

Rain falling, glistening in the moonlight. A loud howl echoed off the mountain. A cabin in the dark, scary woods. A black figure waved harmlessly in the old, dusty window. A blink of an eye gone. A loud creak as the door opened behind me. A cold hand on my shoulder. I floated to the ceiling. A bright white flash. *Bang!* I hit the cold wooden floor. Above me, a dark, mysterious figure.

Ben Calvo (15)
St George's CE School, Gravesend

The Bloody Hospital

As I enter the hospital, I see lights flickering on and off. Blood being spilt from the broken ceiling. I look to my right and see a wooden sign, covered with layers of blood. It says: *Beware, you shall not pass*. I go around the corner, shivering my way through and see a knife jabbed into a wall along with a body hanging. Out of the blue, a vicious woman holding a knife, trying to stab me. I have good reflexes and stop her. I grab a knife from a wall and kill her. The hospital is now safe!

Rohan Janjuha (13)
St George's CE School, Gravesend

Psycho Surgeon

Lights flickering on and off as blood is dripping from the ceiling. I look to my right and see, *Beware, beware, the surgeon is near* on a sign on the wall. I go around the corner and see a dangling body with no legs hanging by a knife through the head. I hear a loud bang. It sounds like a gun. I go further to investigate, only to find my best friend's body on the floor. Suddenly, I hear a gun reload and a deep voice say, 'Welcome to your deathbed!'
Bang!

James Darren Calver (13)
St George's CE School, Gravesend

The Two-Headed Wolves and Hunters In The Wind

Roar! I heard coming from one of the graves. As I walked along the graveyard, I heard a scream. 'Argh!' It was a full moon. I ran into the abandoned church next to the graveyard and heard a howl. It sounded like a werewolf. For the first time all the dogs in Springfield were silent. The legend of the two-headed wolves was true. I began to cry because I was standing at the exact spot where they were killed, thinking this was my last day on Earth. I could hear some mysterious creature crawling towards me. 'Goodbye,' I murmured.

Oluwajoba Kukoyi (15)
St George's CE School, Gravesend

The Depths

Dark... maybe too dark, yet it felt natural. I felt alive, which is strange for a soul so dead. The girls were different to any I had ever encountered, yet they looked so similar. I took one last look at the scars on my body and made the decision. As I levitated closer, I saw my reflection in the top window. For the first time I felt scared, as I finally touched that window, my life flashed before me. I then realised as I looked to either side of me... these girls were a species of very unfriendly demons. Death.

John Bullen (14)
St George's CE School, Gravesend

Toilet Of Terror

It was break time. I was telling a story. One quiet afternoon after school, a boy was walking down the corridor. Suddenly, he heard footsteps behind. They were getting closer and closer. *Bang!* He got dragged into two brown cupboards in the toilets. To this day he sits up in there.

The next week his brother goes to the toilet and looks in the mirror. In the corner he sees his brother. He screams, 'Watch out, you're next!' To this day the boy sits up in the cupboard waiting for his brother to return to the toilet.

HENRY SLACK (14)
St George's CE School, Gravesend

Faceless Man

Every night he appeared within my dreams. The burnt flesh barely covered his skull and would disable any movement from my stiff, paralysed body. The flickering street light would dim at the same time as the synchronised screams would shatter my windows, just before the musky stench of his perspiration would suffocate my room. A wet feeling would tickle my body and the stale smell of blood would burn my nostrils. I could feel my blood-covered body draw the faceless man closer and closer. Schizophrenic shrieks filled my room once again. My eyes opened, he was on my bed...

JASMINE HOLMES (17)
St George's CE School, Gravesend

A Walk Among The Tombstones

It was 11:58 and my journey home from work was tiresome. Every night I would dart through the masses of headstones, weaving in and out of them like a frenzied animal. But tonight the fog was suspended in the air, so thick it looked unnatural. It was sub-zero temperatures so my limbs were stiff, unwilling to move. The silence was deafening so when the scream came, it was ear-piercing. I felt my heart palpitate and sink into my stomach. Suddenly, I was paralysed...

CHLOE WALKER (18)
St George's CE School, Gravesend

Aberration?

On the hill within the moors is where no one would dare to venture. Tales of ghouls, ghosts and wolves was the ever present talk that shadowed the town, but I was not scared. Battling with trees, spooks and fog that thickened the air, I wandered into the mist of the unknown. A chilling shiver shot down my spine as I heard a shriek. My mind was playing tricks no less. A howl echoed as I felt a hand that wasn't visible, I ran for cover, only to stumble. I hit the ground, frozen by the stare of a girl.

JADE-FURNESS MILLER (17)
St George's CE School, Gravesend

The Haunted House

Once upon a time there was a big haunted house that three boys always visited. Their names were Charlie, Jamie and Harry. They weren't scared of anything, until one day something strange happened in that big, dark, haunted house that had actually never happened before. Charlie, Jamie and Harry didn't really know what to do. Let me tell you what happened...

They were walking and then suddenly, the floor dropped. They fell down and it took them to another level of the haunted house. There was a big black thing chasing them. They fell unconscious. That was the end.

Harry Aldum (13)
The Hundred of Hoo Academy, Rochester

Untitled

I stumbled blindly through the forest, tripping over every twig and stick. However, as I was beginning to lose all hope of finding a place to hide, I suddenly saw beams of light flood the forest floor. Intrigued, I wandered over to the light, only to discover a dead body. The person was cut and slashed and blood oozed out of him like lava from a volcano. Suddenly, thoughts took over my mind, I wondered if the people who were hunting me had killed this person. But why? Also, how much time did I have until I could quickly escape?

Robert Pankhurst (13)
The Hundred of Hoo Academy, Rochester

THE TRANSFORMATION SAGA

My heart tap danced inside my ribs. 'Who's there?' I screamed, but no answer returned. Suddenly, a swift pain scratched my shoulder. My arm became a blood waterfall. I slowly dropped to the damp ground. I watched in shock as a pale figure emerged from the darkness, its hand soaked in blood (my blood). As it came closer to me, an intense coldness grew with it. It smiled at me, revealing its long, sharp fangs. It began to intimidatingly kneel down, those blood-red eyes never stopped staring into mine, paralysing my mind. It began to lean forward... pain followed...

SHANNON MACHIN (13)
The Hundred of Hoo Academy, Rochester

HAUNTED HOUSE

It got harder to see in the fog. The little boy riding his bike bumped into a mysterious-looking house in the middle of the woods. He then went in it to see if anyone was in. The little boy felt something crawl up his back. He went to check what it was and it was all slimy and gooey. He screamed and tried to run away, but someone grabbed him. He turned to his left, then his right. He saw a ghost with slime dripping off the ghost holding an axe, ready to cut off his head...

YASMIN MILLS (12)
The Hundred of Hoo Academy, Rochester

DEAD OR ALIVE?

It was a cold, dark November night. Lady Jenna was at home listening to the wind that blew through the trees. She heard the letterbox rattle. There, on the mat, was a letter. She read it. She froze in terror. It was from her dead husband, Jacob, asking to meet her. She ran to the graveyard and began digging up the coffin. She opened the lid and stared in disbelief. The coffin was empty. Was her husband really dead or was someone trying to mess with her mind after all these years? The lights flickered. *Bang!* It all went dark...

JOSHUA CHERRY (11)
The Hundred of Hoo Academy, Rochester

THE SCHOOLGIRL

Our shadows are dispersed. But see how our fingers tremble. Fingers and hands tangled. We break forward like fighters. It's been a long time since I've seen myself in the mirror, but I know my transparent complexion frightens even the brave. Some might call this prejudice, I call it fear. It's the black voice at the back of your mind that niggles your head. I see the scars across my wrist. I loom around my school, desperate to be noticed but the pupils don't see me. They only read about me, talk about me. I don't miss the despair.

GEORGIA ERIN MCINTOSH (13)
The Hundred of Hoo Academy, Rochester

THE MAN

One stormy night, there in the corner, stood a man. Suddenly, he disappeared.

The next day two children went to a graveyard. However, they didn't realise Joe was standing by a tree watching them. 'Good day, little girls. How do you do?' Joe asked.

'Mummy told us not to talk to strangers,' the littlest girl replied, then walked off.

A week later, Joe kidnapped the girls and took them to an old, abandoned farmyard. He whispered, 'I have only taken you because you are young and beautiful, and I want you for myself as my own children.'

SARAH-JAYNE MURPHY (11)
The Hundred of Hoo Academy, Rochester

THE BEAST HOUSE

In the middle of nowhere stood an abandoned building covered in an ashy substance with smashed windows. A graveyard in the distance covered in cobwebs and dust. Bones lying above the mud. A huge wall surrounded the house as if it were the moat of a castle. Joe climbed over the wall and started to walk up the grass towards the house. He got about one metre away from the house when the grass started to gobble him up like a monster. He tried to pull himself out of the grass. With every attempt, he sank further into the grass...

IMOGEN MUNDAY (12)
The Hundred of Hoo Academy, Rochester

THE WINDOW

The fog was creeping up to the haunted mansion. Vines grew up all over. It had been abandoned for years and it was in the middle of nowhere. It was known to be haunted. Apparently, if you go out at quarter past three, you can see the woman and the little man in the window with the lights flashing. I went out to see it. I set an alarm and I went. I got there and the lights were flashing. I watched in my car then turned the engine on and sped back home.

LOUIS PETER HAPPY (11)
The Hundred of Hoo Academy, Rochester

BACKPACKING

It was late, dark and eerie. I had wandered from the group. I was now alone in the woods. As I strained my eyes to see a pathway, I saw a figure in the distance. I started to run towards them, thinking they were a friend. I was wrong. Its grin widened and its eyes lit up like a street lamp on a foggy evening. I stopped dead in my tracks. As I started stepping back, its arms elongated and reached me, pulling me closer. It whispered, 'Join the wanderers.'

HARRISON COLLINS (13)
The Hundred of Hoo Academy, Rochester

THE DARK

Pain shot through my leg. I couldn't see anything, the silence drowned me. I could feel blood trickling down my leg. Scrambling up, I could see the faint silhouette of a woman standing looking at me. Her eyes were bloodshot and her teeth yellow with age. She giggled, but not a sweet child's giggle, no, a croaky, menacing laugh that sent shivers down my spine. Lightning flashed across the room. Her face was disturbing. 'Peekaboo,' she screamed, running towards me. She grabbed my leg. I kicked and thrashed, but she was too strong. She dragged me back into the dark...

ELLIE MCNAMARA (14)
The Hundred of Hoo Academy, Rochester

THE SHADOW IN THE DARKNESS

Silence drowned me. The only sounds I heard were my fear-filled, beating heart as well as the gentle tapping of my shoes. The black, silky abyss enveloped my whole body. All of a sudden, a light flickered ahead of me. Something was there. The shadowy figure swayed slowly. My eyes fixated on the... 'thing'. A slow gargling could be heard. I stepped closer towards it. My heart raced. As I drew close, the lights suddenly burst. I stood still in the darkness. My eyes slowly adjusted. Something loomed close. The stench of its breath was rotten. 'I can see you... '

CHEYENNE HENDRICK (14)
The Hundred of Hoo Academy, Rochester

THE DARK FIGURE

Bang! The pistol shot. My legs fell to the floor. I couldn't move. The dark figure was walking closer and closer to me. The shadowed hands reached before me. I screamed! The dark figure was no longer there. It had disappeared, as if it had vanished! Where could this thing have gone? It was behind me! There was no escaping for me! I was finished. I was dead!

KAYLEIGH ANNE-MARIE CHANDLER (12)
The Hundred of Hoo Academy, Rochester

NOTHING

I sat there staring into space, waiting for something, anything, to happen. It was getting dark but I still sat there waiting for something to happen. Sure, it was boring but it was still better than being at home. As I kept daydreaming, a gust of wind flew across my face. At that moment, nothing happened. Just after, I heard screeching noises coming from behind me. Then when I looked behind me, there was nothing. Quickly, after that I thought I could see a dead body, but when I shone a light on it, there was nothing...

HARRY JOHNSON (12)
The Hundred of Hoo Academy, Rochester

THE CHINA DOLL

Within the depths of the silent graveyard sat a haunted church.
The church was wrapped in a thick mist. A girl called Jennifa was a
curious girl.
One stormy night when the lightning was striking the ground, Jennifa
went to the graveyard. As she trudged along the squelching mud,
Jennifa saw the church looming in the fog. Trekking over to the
gloomy church, she saw some blood trails leading up to the church
steps. With a great heave, Jennifa pushed into the door to find a
china doll bleeding from the eyes. 'Hi!' screeched the doll.
'Argh!' screamed Jennifa...

SOPHIE SPARKS (11)
The Hundred of Hoo Academy, Rochester

THE MYSTERIOUS DEATH

Jane called for her brother. No reply. She went and sat down. When
she called his number, it started ringing. The ringing was coming
from the basement. When she went down, she discovered her
brother's body. She felt a cold hand brush against her back. She
could hear the water colliding over the road where the sea was.
At her brother's funeral, she went for a walk. She thought she saw
her brother but he disappeared. She felt sad. She wished her brother
was there. The wind and rain picked up slowly. If she had paid
attention, she'd have survived.

REECE JIMMY FIDDYMENT (12)
The Hundred of Hoo Academy, Rochester

THE MOONLIT GRAVEYARD

Macy pushed the creaking gate open and entered the haunted graveyard. Gravestones lined up like soldiers at attention. The breeze made the bare trees rustle and twigs crack. The chilly air gave Macy tingles down her spine, making her blood run cold. The eerie silence flooded the graveyard, not even the sound of cracking sticks could be heard. Tentatively, Macy pulled out her mobile phone and called her friend, Amy. Amy was supposed to meet Macy at the graveyard, but she was five minutes late. Then Macy felt a cold, bony hand clutch her shoulder suddenly. Slowly, she turned around...

REBECCA GOODWIN (11)
The Hundred of Hoo Academy, Rochester

SKANKY STREET

It was Friday 13th and I believe that it's not a bad day. I came home from school and it was going fine until I walked down the most disgusting street. I hate walking down this street, it gets so dark when it is 4 o'clock. I took about 30 steps. I ran for my life. Everything alive was looking at me. This might be the end. I was running out of breath. Things were coming after me. I got so scared but in front of me was my mum's car and her. My heart rose in relief. 'Mum!'

AARON TURNER (13)
The Hundred of Hoo Academy, Rochester

Midnight Walk

Bang! The oak wooden door clattered in-between the door frame. I looked back at the door, feeling suspicious. I felt like someone was tipping -30° ice cubes down my back. As I turned with fear, a gust of wind passed me. *Creak!* The floorboards creaked as if they'd just been beaten. The wooden interior of the haunted house smelt damp. The wooden banister felt cold and as if I was stroking my hand against a long, slithery, wet snake.

As I reached the top of the oak stairs, two passageways led to the right and left...

Harvey Scott Green (13)
The Hundred of Hoo Academy, Rochester

The Winding Clock

Standing straight on a mantelpiece slowly piling up with dust, stood one old clock just waiting to be found. Luckily, that day soon came. Two young people found it and took it in their tiny hands. But now they weren't so young anymore, they had reached their old age and they still had the clock. But it began to get slower every day and the man that wound the clock every day had got cancer. He got weaker and weaker. It became night and the man died. The time he died, the clock stopped.

Lauren Battelle (13)
The Hundred of Hoo Academy, Rochester

Hello...

'Hello... ' I whispered as the antiquated door slowly creaked open. There was no reply. Reluctantly, I walked towards the door, oblivious of the consequences that were coming my way. Nobody was to be seen. However, I had an instinct that I was not alone. *Bang! Crash!* The pans from above the stove immediately crashed onto the floor. I was horrified but I couldn't help but look. I crept over to the kitchen with nothing to find but a note on the table stating, 'Turn around'. Slowly, I turned around, only to find several knives in my chest. 'Hello... ' he said.

SOMMER BRIDGE (12)
The Hundred of Hoo Academy, Rochester

Untitled

Once upon a time there was a very dark forest and in that dark forest there was a big, scary, mossy house that had not been touched for 1,000 years. No one entered.
One day, a girl called Emily fancied an adventure and decided to enter the house! There were rumours that the house was haunted. But she did not believe it. She thought that ghosts and ghouls were not real and nor were vampires and monsters. So she had nothing to stop her from going in there. So she stepped into the building and... *boom!*

NIAMH HUNT (11)
The Hundred of Hoo Academy, Rochester

What Was It?

The day had been fine considering it was Friday the 13th. Mum had asked me to go to the shops. I don't know what I was worrying about, they're just superstitions. However, the street lamps flickered. I thought nothing of it. There wasn't a soul in sight. Fog chased me to the shop. I began to worry. I looked through the shop window. No one there. In the reflection, I saw something coming through the fog. My mouth became dry, my hands sweaty...
I ran through the graveyard with fog chasing. Whatever it was, it was chasing me, breathing heavily.

JOSEPH WELFORD (13)
The Hundred of Hoo Academy, Rochester

The Lost Creature

Long, long ago in an abandoned temple, lived a creature who had never been seen. The basilisk! Nobody had an idea where it lived, except me! Once I visited the temple. It looked nothing like I imagined. I thought it would be mossy, dirty and stinky. It was white. 'Hello!' I yelled. 'Is anyone there?' Nobody answered. I was so creeped out, I wanted to leave but the way I came in was blocked. A rock fell and nearly hit me on my head. I'll tell all of my friends once I get away from the basilisk, alive.

LILY-MAE TAPPENDEN (11)
The Hundred of Hoo Academy, Rochester

UNTITLED

Ruby went to the graveyard to see her grandad. She stayed there until 8pm. It was winter and pitch-black. Then she heard someone in the distance. The lights flickered on and off for half an hour. In the distance she saw a man. He sat next to her and said, 'Rough time, eh?'
Ruby said, 'Yes, I've been sitting here for the last seven hours!'
He said, 'I know how you feel.'
Then she realised something. It was her teacher from school. 'Sir, what are you doing here?'
He said, 'I was trying to find you.'

JODIE JEMMA WENBOURNE (13)
The Hundred of Hoo Academy, Rochester

THE RED DEVIL

Bang! The door was slammed. 'Who's there?' I screamed. No one answered. I couldn't move or scream out for help. But I knew someone was there. I could see their shadow in the moonlight. I managed to move my arm and tried to find a torch in my bedside cabinet. I got out a torch and shone it at the door. '*Argh!*' I screamed. There was a person standing there dressed in a red-horned devil costume wielding a knife. '*Argh!*' Silence came from the room...

AMBER FAGENCE (13)
The Hundred of Hoo Academy, Rochester

The Mansion

The door creaked open, revealing the inside of the abandoned mansion. Cobwebs hung from the ceiling like ropes. The floorboards moaned under my feet. Dust lay like a sheet of snow concealing everything in its path. I walked down the dark hallway; the lights flickered. But the power was off... I started to panic and ran as fast as I could. I stopped. I had lost myself within this abandoned place. With the lights still flickering, I slowly turned around. I stopped dead in my tracks as I felt an icy-cold hand on my shoulder. I screamed...

Orla Grady (13)
The Hundred of Hoo Academy, Rochester

Screams

The lamps flickered eerily as I approached the nearby graveyard. Screams pierced the silence abruptly, the echo carried it on. Was I the only one who could hear them? Still I moved forwards as if possessed. Tears began to fall down my face that I had no control over. Fierce wind whipped across my face as I slowly moved forward. Shouts and pleas came louder than I could bear. Rain pelted down, making me so cold that I was now numb. My knees gave way as I tumbled to the floor. That's when I realised the screams were my own.

Bethany Small (14)
The Hundred of Hoo Academy, Rochester

THE ALLEY

I left the building and started walking down the alley. The lights were flickering and alley cats were scavenging for food remains in bins. I carried on walking, knowing that all sounds around me were just noises coming from houses nearby. But there was one sound that I had never heard in this alley before. It was footsteps and they weren't mine. I turned around and there was no one there, just a poor little cat with nothing to eat. I reached into my little leather bag and pulled out some food. I carried on walking. Footsteps came again...

JIMMY-DEAN ROBERTS (14)
The Hundred of Hoo Academy, Rochester

THE TENT OF DESPAIR

The house lights flickered constantly and only the super moon gave constant light on her street. Polly galloped down the street to the big, stripy tent. What was inside? What would she find? She heard Garland Entree playing and she knew where she was. She saw a clown. She saw a ringmaster. She saw the circus. The ringmaster said, 'Any volunteers?' No one volunteered. So they picked someone. They shouted to Polly several times. They grabbed her. She screamed! She screeched! She cried! She fell to the floor! All she knew was she had an immense and terrifying nightmare.

AMELIA COTTLE (13)
The Hundred of Hoo Academy, Rochester

Death's Gate

The door creaked as I entered the smoky graveyard. The smell of death lurked behind every tree. As I walked past the headstones, I noticed a hole in the ground. A body should be in that hole, but it wasn't. I headed for the graveyard's exit when a dark figure blocked my path. I ran the other way, desperate to get out. I was surrounded by many, many more dark figures. They were closing in on me, getting closer and closer. Then that was it. The last thing I remember before who I am today... a monster!

Kira-May Dobbs (12)
The Hundred of Hoo Academy, Rochester

The Ouija Board

It was cold and gloomy. The wind smashed through the cracks in the window whilst the wolf howled at the full moon and spirits awoke from their slumber. I'd chosen the perfect night to do the Ouija boa-... *Bang!* The old, rotting door flew open and the Ouija board smashed onto the cold, hard floor! The spirits did not want me doing the Ouija board because they knew who I was trying to reach on the other side and that was one of my great ancestors... Jack! My family's most hated serial killer of all time!

Gracie Miller (12)
The Hundred of Hoo Academy, Rochester

Untitled

Once there was a man who lost his best friend. Seven years after that, he became a miserable old man.

One night, the old man heard chains jingling and boxes hitting the ground. Then the door handle slowly moved to the left, then to the right. The dim lights flickered, then the old door creaked as it opened slightly. It swung open, then a white, hovering man came out of the black room. As the ghost entered the dimly lit room, the old man shouted, 'Who are you?' There was no reply, to the old man's horror.

SOPHIA FARMER (12)
The Hundred of Hoo Academy, Rochester

THE GIRLS THAT WERE NEVER SEEN AGAIN

In a school of girls, there was a mystery wardrobe at the back of the upstairs corridor that no one ever went near. The last time someone went near it, they were never to be seen again. Suddenly, one stormy day, two girls, Skye and Emily, saw the wardrobe shaking and the doors began to open. They then heard a voice inside. They walked closer and closer to the wardrobe and out spoke a voice, 'Come in to the wardrobe of fun.' Emily and Skye were arguing whether to go in or not. Then suddenly, a hand pulled them in...

KATHERINE AMANDA LAMB (12)
The Hundred of Hoo Academy, Rochester

THE CREEPY HOUSE!

There was a house in the middle of the woods. No one ever went in and if they did, they didn't come out. But one strange day, a boy started to hear voices inside the house saying, 'Come in.' He decided to enter the house. As he entered, more voices said, 'Come up the stairs.' So he did. He opened a door. All he could see was a girl on a chair singing a creepy song. She started chasing him. As he reached outside, he got dragged back and he was never seen again. Nobody goes in anymore!

TYLER GOUGH (13)
The Hundred of Hoo Academy, Rochester

THE SPOOKY CHURCH

One night, there were three kids at an old-looking church and there was a big graveyard. There were loads and loads of graves on the ground, so they went home and came back in daylight. They went into the church and heard the door shut behind them. There was a voice saying, 'Let me free.' They didn't know where it was coming from. They heard it and saw who it was. It was their friend.
It soon got dark. They opened the door and they never went back ever again.

REECE NICHOLAS PAY (13)
The Hundred of Hoo Academy, Rochester

Untitled

It's dark, I'm alone. It's getting hard to breathe. The walls grow closer with every step. The only light is through the crack in the window. On the other side of the street I hear footsteps, laughter and the sound of someone calling me. It is a harsh, sharp voice. It's digging into my brain. I stagger towards it, hoping for it to be real. 'Help!' My mind is going crazy. I am seeing things, hearing things. I sit on the pavement, hoping for help to go by. I wait and wait, but no one comes. I'm stuck...

Brandon Robinson (13)
The Hundred of Hoo Academy, Rochester

The Darkness

As I look around, it looks like the walls are getting closer. People are ignoring me as I crawl into a ball in the tight corner, I feel sudden movements on my body. Darkness is coming, very quickly. I pull and grab my keys. The lights flicker then go. It's now dark. I can hear screams of victims taken by the darkness. Is it a thing or a shadow? Am I imagining things? I walk to my door and *slam!* I collapse to the ground and hear a faint, dark voice saying, 'You can't hide from me, I've awoken!'

Bradley Ahmet (13)
The Hundred of Hoo Academy, Rochester

Sarah's Nightmare

It was a full moon night and it was Halloween, the most scary night. On that night, Sarah went to bed at 7 o'clock, not because she wanted but because she was scared. The big windows in her bedroom opened and a strong wind came in. Sarah screamed. She cried and shouted really loud. Very slowly, she walked through her bedroom and when she looked through the window, everyone was dead. She thought that it was a dream, so she went to bed. The next morning there was no one. She was the only person in the world.

Ana Luis (13)
The Hundred of Hoo Academy, Rochester

Snap

It was lifeless in the woods. *Snap!* Joe looked around him. The trees were clawing at his head as he cautiously wandered down the path. The trees seemed to be winding into each other, making Joe feel very frightened but he pushed the thought away. Joe felt a sudden chill trickle up his spine. He froze. Silence lurked around him. Then, in the distance, a mutter came. Joe was positive no one was there or ever was there. He started walking, then running, and finally sprinting. Out of breath, Joe stopped. *Snap! Snap! Snap!* Suddenly, something grabbed his leg...

Jodie Lee (12)
The Hundred of Hoo Academy, Rochester

THE SLENDER SHADOW

The street was cold and dark. My ragged breathing was the only sound in the deserted street. The street lamp up ahead flickered and blew out in a frenzy of sparks in all directions. The shower lasted so quickly, it burned my eyes and a strange man appeared from nowhere. He was tall and slender. As I stepped back, startled, I took in so much more. He was wearing a suit of black and a tie of red. All the light had gone and my path was blocked by him. So I ran, with the man in hot pursuit.

MASON WHITE (13)
The Hundred of Hoo Academy, Rochester

ZOMBIE!

Bang! My heart thumped in my chest like a hammer destroying my lungs. I shrieked in fear as I sprinted from the depths of my basement to escape from the zombie! I could hear its moaning rasping from its mouth! Horrified, I stumbled out of my house and dashed to the street where hundreds of zombies infested the whole town! I grabbed a bone I found on the floor and struck the zombies with it. I turned around and gazed into the darkness of the street. Out came another zombie and it sank its teeth into me...

BEN FOX (13)
The Hundred of Hoo Academy, Rochester

THE DAUNTING

One by one, step by step, we go closer to our fears. I clenched my hand on the edge of the door knob and twisted at a 90° angle. My heartbeat got louder, yet weaker by each second. The door blew wide open and nothing was to be seen except the shadow of him. The shadow was tall, wore a black hat and stood straight in freedom. The howl echoed through the wind at a ghostly speed. My heart dropped, no thought, just silence, for I had realised the man standing right in front of me was my uncle.

GEORGIA CLABON (13)
The Hundred of Hoo Academy, Rochester

FRANK AND THE FOG DWELLER

One dark and misty night, Frank was walking home after leaving his night shift. The fog had rolled in unexpectedly as he saw through the screen of his surveillance cameras he'd sat in front of since 9pm. It was now 2am and even though the eerie emptiness of the old pizzeria place was tough enough, he now wished he was back... at least he could see everything. The fog was so thick he could hardly see his feet, and the silence caused the ringing in his ears to be deafening. Sadly, this prevented him hearing the footsteps behind him...

LUKE GAY (13)
The Hundred of Hoo Academy, Rochester

UNTITLED

Lamp posts flickered down the dull, dark, spooky street. I edged up the road, constantly looking behind me, but it was no use, the fog had followed me and surrounded me. I could no longer see where I was going, not even the lamp posts were visible. I picked up the pace, running into the unknown. I heard a growl echo around me as I came to a stop. The fog cleared. Before my eyes was the graveyard. I fell to the ground with a thump. Before I knew it, I was lying in the mud, alone.

CALLUM BUSSEY (13)
The Hundred of Hoo Academy, Rochester

DARKNESS

Darkness filled the room. There was no escape from what was coming. A man stood in the darkness. His tall figure was all I could make out. 'He will rise again!' was all he said. Then I woke up in sweats. Suddenly, there was a loud *bang!* on the door. Shaking, I opened it. There was the man from my dream. I thought, hoped, that I was still dreaming and that I would wake up soon. However, the man at the door didn't leave and I didn't wake up. The tall man pulled an object out of his pocket...

GRACE ARTERTON (12)
The Hundred of Hoo Academy, Rochester

Untitled

Bang! The axe from the armour stand fell and nearly chopped Kristina into a million pieces. She turned around and saw a malfunctioning animatronic holding a match in one hand and a lighter in the other. She ran out of the door of the haunted mansion and watched as the animatronic ballistically set the mansion on fire. She watched anxiously as the building and furniture slowly burnt to ashes. But where was the animatronic? Was he alive? Was he dead? Did he escape? Or was it only a dream?

FAITH MAHONEY (12)
The Hundred of Hoo Academy, Rochester

Monstrous

In a very dark town, in a very dark street, in a very dark house lived a grotesque monster who ate the flesh of humans. It lived under beds, wardrobes, attics and fridges. It had red eyes and a black tongue. One day, a boy went to this particular house to show he was not afraid, but he was shaking and all you heard was a scream with a bone crunch. It was spine-chilling. What happened to him? No one knows, but he never came out to see daylight again. For your sake, don't go there!

MATTHEW POPOV (11)
The Hundred of Hoo Academy, Rochester

GHOST HUNTER

Crack! The lightning flashed before my eyes. I entered the dark, cold house. It was meant to be haunted with a terrifying ghost, the king of all ghosts, King Henry VIII's ghost!
I heard a woman's scream. It was an ear-splitting scream, it almost made my ears bleed. It wasn't a scream of fear, but of pain. I almost felt her pain with the scream. It dug into me, pierced me, frightened me, but I wouldn't let that scream get in my way, no matter how much it hurt. I would get that ghost. Nothing would stop me!

KRISTINA MOLLINS (11)
The Hundred of Hoo Academy, Rochester

THE HAUNTED HOUSE

One spooky night, the clouds were grey and there was thunder. In the evening, a girl named Abbey found a spooky house. She thought in her mind that this looked definitely like a haunted house. She was scared and was about to walk away when she heard a strange noise. It was a noisy, creaky sound. She noticed that the door had opened. She looked back behind her and ran as fast as she could home. When she got home, she told her mum all about what happened when she was walking home from the park.

CHLOE SEAMAN (11)
The Hundred of Hoo Academy, Rochester

The Boy's Prank

Crash! The book fell. I turned to see a dark, narrow corridor. At the end, a tall man stood with something in his hands. I screamed in shock. Next thing I knew, I was getting dragged down the stairs, not knowing what to do. The front door flew open as more dark figures flooded into my house. I wondered what they were doing and why they were taking me. They kept on dragging me out the front door. My clothes were getting holes in them and my hands were getting grazed. I recognised my surroundings. I was at my friend's house.

Jack South (13)
The Hundred of Hoo Academy, Rochester

The Mansion

The floorboards creaked as Armin stood, paralysed. They were slowly approaching him. He didn't know who, but they were coming. Large, heavy footsteps echoed around the dilapidated mansion, the source being in the room across the hallway from Armin. His heart began racing faster than the wings of a hummingbird but his curiosity overcame his fear and forced him to investigate. Slowly, he crept along, trying his hardest not to make a sound. As he was only a few feet from the door, he heard something shift around and through the crack, he saw a single bloodshot eye...

Josh Cronin (14)
The Hundred of Hoo Academy, Rochester

Followed

On the way to the party, I saw something or someone following me. I walked faster and faster, but it was still behind me. Whilst it was following me, two more people or animals joined it. When I was almost at the party, two men stopped in front of me. Then they pulled out guns and aimed them at the things behind me. But just then, a van pulled up and they threw me into it, putting a bag on my head. Whilst I was in the van, I heard gunshots and screams...

Ian Titmuss (13)
The Hundred of Hoo Academy, Rochester

Untitled

Flicker, went the lamps. *Bang!* went the doors of the trick or treaters. They all went to sleep, all but one. A car's headlights turned round the corner from where the trick or treater sat. He saw the car and ran. He left the candy behind. The car followed. He continued to run till he got to his house. The car turned off. The boy was unlocking the door of his house as a man got out of the car. The boy's mum opened the door when she heard a scream. The boy and the car were gone!

Sean Soper
The Hundred of Hoo Academy, Rochester

BANG!

I was sitting in a café having a bowl of mushroom soup with bread. The café was old-fashioned and had been there for a long time. When I was just about to slurp the last of my soup, I heard a *bang!* I took no notice of it until... there was a bigger bang! I hid under the table, then about five people with black masks said, 'Get down or someone will get hurt!' Then they kept shooting next to me. *Bang! Bang!* I heard someone scream. They were dead! Then there was another bang! They were gone!

HARRY KENT
The Hundred of Hoo Academy, Rochester

THE CLOWN

I just got back from a new, famous circus. It was dark and only a couple of street lights were on. I ran in the house. I went straight to the bathroom and looked in the mirror. I saw a clown in it. I rubbed my eyes, then it disappeared. I was scared. Was I being haunted or was I just seeing things? I didn't know. A bang! A thud! What was that? *I'm just hearing things. Maybe it was the neighbours. Yeah, it was them, they are always noisy.*
'Arrgghh! Help me, he's going to kill me! Help! Noooo... '

GEORGE TURNER (13)
The Hundred of Hoo Academy, Rochester

A Surprise

The room was dark. The thin air made it hard to breathe. The blood dripped down the wall like a child squeezing a juice box. The long, jagged knife tipped off the table. The long outline of what seemed to be a body lying on the bed. The grey smoke rising from the carpet like from a cigarette. The blood-soaked clothes on the floor; but Jack still went, kept walking, heart racing until he saw it. The green feet, the ripped jeans, the blood-soaked shirt and finally, the green head with metal sticking out of it. The Frankenstein.

EZEKIEL AKINSANYA (12)
The Hundred of Hoo Academy, Rochester

Full Moon

It was a stormy night. Lights flickered as trees swayed side to side. As I moved slowly towards my father's grave, there was a horrific sound in the distance. 'Help!' There it was again. 'Help!' I ran, I fell. With the full moon beaming down on me, I wondered what was out there, probably looking at me from afar. Then a noise from the distance, 'Go away!' I quickly got up, turned around and there was something tall in front of me. As I rolled my eyes up, the face of a monster stared at me.

WILLIAM ALLAN JOHN LAMB (14)
The Hundred of Hoo Academy, Rochester

THE ZOMBIE CHICKEN

As I walked slowly in the dark gloomy forest, I was lost and alone. I just kept on walking and walking in the dark and I heard the *snap* of a stick. I looked back to see nothing, then I turned back around. I saw the most terrifying thing in my life, it was green and wrinkly. It had red evil eyes and slime was dripping out of its mouth onto the floor. It was massive, it was the zombie chicken! *Bwark! Bwark! Bwark! Bwark!* went the zombie chicken.

'Aaarrgghh!' I screamed. That was the scariest thing I've ever seen!

SAMUEL JOHNSON (11)
The Hundred of Hoo Academy, Rochester

UNTITLED

One night, on Friday the 13th July, Jessica was sound asleep in her single pink bed, when she heard a loud bang coming from her brother's room. Jessica slowly went out of her room and walked towards the door. It creaked. She stopped for a moment, then opened it quickly, not caring about the noise. Just then... she heard the front door open, then close. Jessica, being terrified still, fled downstairs and came across her brother on the floor and her dad standing over him with a knife. Jessica's dad looked up at her and walked forward...

LAUREN HAZELL (11)
The Hundred of Hoo Academy, Rochester

THE BLOODY HORROR!

It was a cold, dark night when the wolves were howling and growling at the moon, while I was walking across a graveyard leading to a creepy, huge church. When I opened the door... *bang!* A water bucket fell on my head (with water in it). Then I heard footsteps. When I turned around... *argh!* It was a murderer with a black mask and a bloody knife. It scared me. I ran all the way to the other side of the church and hid. After a while, he disappeared, so I crept out...
I wonder what happened to the murderer?

KATIE BAKER (12)
The Hundred of Hoo Academy, Rochester

HAUNTED MANSION

A little girl was lost in a forest. She saw a little hut and lots of bats. The bats started to attack her. She ran straight into a haunted mansion. She spotted a mask that was moving around. She went to exit, but something was walking down the staircase. It was Jason the killer with a Samurai sword with his killer dog and his brother. They started running at the little girl. She knew she was going to die, so she just let them kill her.

JOSHUA BLAKE FLETCHER (11)
The Hundred of Hoo Academy, Rochester

THE GRAB

It was an average house, in an average street, in a neighbourhood filled with average people. But behind the door lurked an evil mystery...

I'm sure I turned that light off. Oh, I can't have. I walked into the kitchen where the knives were arranged on the counter. 'Hi,' I shouted. 'Yes?' she shouted back.

'Nothing.' Then I stopped and turned at the bottom of the stairs. Something grabbed my throat. *'Argh!'* I screamed as I was dragged up the stairs, viciously. It clawed at my throat with invisible hands. 'Get out... now!' whispered a voice in my ear.

JESSICA MORLEY (11)
The Hundred of Hoo Academy, Rochester

UNTITLED

As I slowly walked up to this pitch-black house, *bang!* A puff of smoke appeared in front of me. I walked a bit more and saw this big, dark and gloomy black house in front of me. I went in to explore. As I walked, I saw something dash past me. I turned my torch on and nervously went to explore. I walked slowly down the hallway into a room. 'Hello!' I yelled. There was no reply. I started to look around and explore. All there was were old chairs and tables. I quickly rushed back home.

GEORGIA CARTER
The Hundred of Hoo Academy, Rochester

FRIENDS FRIGHT

One night, me and my friend, Lilly, went to a dead church. We heard spooky, scary skeletons and had shivers down our spines. We heard growling from zombies. Lilly found us a pistol each. Ghosts were everywhere. Lilly said, 'Who you gonna call? Ghost Busters.' It made me laugh.

Freddy Krueger was scratching at the door. *Boom!* The doors came down. Lilly and me killed all of the zombies. We had a boss battle, me and Lilly versus Freddy. He tried killing Lilly, but I saved her. Me and Lilly kicked Freddy Krueger's stupid, silly butt, then we had cake.

HANNAH FORD (11)
The Hundred of Hoo Academy, Rochester

UNTITLED

A flow of cold air drifted through the door and sent shivers down her spine. She felt the presence of someone else. The rusty old door began to creak and it suddenly slammed shut. She was trapped! In the dark, all alone, or was she? She tried to escape but there was no way out. The creature followed her. It was nowhere to be seen but it was definitely with her. Her heart was thumping fast. Was she going to survive? She screamed, hoping someone would hear her, but no one was around. How was she going to escape now?

GEORGIA LEE (13)
The Hundred of Hoo Academy, Rochester

When I Was At My Nan's

My nan died. My nan and I were so close we'd tell each other everything, from dogs to death.

I went to her house. It was cold, very cold. As I opened the green, wooden, rustic door, there was no welcome, just silence. There was no sweet smell of cinnamon and none of Pudge's hair around. Dust filled my nose. I started clearing out things, quietly. Music, the record player, a tune from the 60s. I looked around, shocked. *Smash!* A picture fell. I needed to get out! The door shut, there was no way out. I was stuck!

Flo Beaver (14)
The Hundred of Hoo Academy, Rochester

Unknown Fear

I had awoken to the sound of children's laughter. I couldn't see anything except for the moon shining through my window. I got up and tried to get to my door in one piece. I opened the door slowly. The screeching of the door startled me. I came to realise someone had entered my house. I could feel the wind drive past my naked legs. I walked downstairs, hearing cupboards banging and cups smashing. I walked into the dining room and my favourite cup rolled past me. I tiptoed into the kitchen. I couldn't believe what I saw...

Joe Wheeldon (13)
The Hundred of Hoo Academy, Rochester

THE CLOWN MASK

A chill shivered up my long, broken spine. As I lay there, worms crawled on my muddy legs. In the distance, I saw a red mask sitting on the bench with a huge grin on its face. I began to get scared. I hobbled over to the old, abandoned bench, but when I looked, the mask had disappeared. Suddenly, I heard a small whisper in my cold ear. It was only then that I knew it was the mask. I screamed! I tried to crawl away but the pain was too much to handle. The mask jumped on my face...

INDIA SEDDON (12)
The Hundred of Hoo Academy, Rochester

THE ZOMBIES

The sky became dark and grim. I shivered with fear as the noise of groaning came closer. I ran towards the old church. The sheer terror of it all was making my heart beat faster. As I ran into the church, the door slammed shut behind me. The light from the full moon shone through the windows, casting eerie shadows around the walls. The church was dusty and cold inside. The wind howled outside. The door started to make a rattling sound. I was petrified and stood frozen like a statue. I felt cold breath on my neck...

DANIEL CHANNING (11)
The Hundred of Hoo Academy, Rochester

The Unknown

Thunder was determined to demolish the day I was petrified to get back home in the pitch-black. I was now face-to-face with the coffins of Sagada, Philippines, not knowing why I was here. For some peculiar reason, I could smell a kind of whipped cream. The volume of the fluttering and tweeting of blackbirds increased. In the chapel, it felt like outside something was moving, moving closer, but what? 'Hello, is anyone there?' I questioned, quite politely. I heard the oxidised door handle open behind me.
'Argh!'

Abinaya Athiththan (11)
The Hundred of Hoo Academy, Rochester

Haunted Cave!

Jim was creeping through the mysterious wet, damp, haunted cave and he felt like he was being watched or, even worse, followed. Jim had been here before. The cave was near his house and he was never allowed in it because of the day Uncle James got murdered. That's why he was not allowed in it. But that did not stop Jim. But there was still someone following him! He turned around, there was no one there. He turned again, nobody. One final time, there was someone there. It was the ghost of Uncle James. *Boo!*

James Bourne (11)
The Hundred of Hoo Academy, Rochester

THE HAUNTED NUTCRACKER

When the Christmas ghouls came out to play, they entered my house, one haunted day. The nutcracker on the shelf was never the same; he moved, he screeched, he played a game. His eyes would follow me around the room, waiting to dish out, my impending doom. I would go out to play and he would glare from behind the holly bush. He followed me around, waiting to see me beneath the ground. He wanted to scare and frighten. Even in the darkest night. I will be keeping on my night light. I hate nutcrackers.

JACK DODD (14)
West Heath School, Sevenoaks

HOUSE OF SECRETS

It was a freezing cold night, the snow was filled with dead animals. I was lost in a petrifying forest where, from a distance, I saw the most spine-chilling house. I knew I had to go in as it was too cold to stay outside. So I moved with trepidation, closer to the house. The door groaned as I went in. I shouted, 'Hello, who's there?' My heart was hammering in my chest with apprehension. Suddenly, I heard a tremendous sound from the distance and a whispering of my name. Then a loud, piercing scream as darkness engulfed me...

ISABELLE STOCKWELL (16)
West Heath School, Sevenoaks

HELP

Once there was a little girl and all she ever wanted was a doll. Her mum said they were too expensive. But she begged so much until her mum went out to get her a doll.

She went to a charity shop and got her rag doll. The little girl knew not to be disrespectful, so she said thank you.

When she awoke the next morning, her family were gone and her doll too. The front door opened and she said, 'There you are.' The doll was there, but she looked like her now...

'Help!'

AARON BIRCH (13)
West Heath School, Sevenoaks

YoungWriters
Est.1991

YOUNG WRITERS INFORMATION

We hope you have enjoyed reading this book – and that you will continue to in the coming years.

If you're a young writer who enjoys reading and creative writing, or the parent of an enthusiastic poet or story writer, do visit our website www.youngwriters.co.uk. Here you will find free competitions, workshops and games, as well as recommended reads, a poetry glossary and our blog.

If you would like to order further copies of this book, or any of our other titles, then please give us a call or visit **www.youngwriters.co.uk.**

Young Writers
Remus House
Coltsfoot Drive
Peterborough
PE2 9BF
(01733) 890066 / 898110
info@youngwriters.co.uk